FREAKY & FEARLESS

The Art of Being a Freak

ROBIN ETHERINGTON

ILLUSTRATED BY JAN BIELECKI

Piccadilly PRESS

First published in Great Britain in 2016 by
PICCADILLY PRESS
80–81 Wimpole St, London W1G 9RE
www.piccadillypress.co.uk

A CIP catalogue record for this book is available from the British
Library.

ISBN: 978-1-8481-2512-4
also available as an ebook

1

Printed and bound by Clays Ltd, St Ives Plc

Piccadilly Press is an imprint of Bonnier Zaffre Ltd,
a Bonnier Publishing company
www.bonnierpublishing.co.uk

FOR LORENZO,
AND OUR LIFETIME SPENT
IN THE FUNNY PAGES
– ROBIN

FOR LENA & KAIA
– JAN

TALES FROM THE TOMB!

IT'S A WELL KNOWN FACT THAT THE MADDEST MAD SCIENTIST OF ALL WAS *IGOR McIGORVICH!*

I SHOULDN'T DRINK THIS . . . BUT I WILL!

NO ONE GUESSED, HOWEVER, THAT A HARMLESS CLAIM WOULD KICKSTART THE END OF THE WORLD.

I'M SMARTER THAN A GOD!! *A GOD!!!*

YEAH? PROVE IT.

PROVE IT HE DID. THE NATURAL WORLD BECAME IGOR'S PLAYTHING . . .

LOOK - A STORM IN A TEACUP!

I'VE MADE A MOUNTAIN FROM A MOLEHILL!

YET ONE CHALLENGE REMAINED . . .

I BET A REAL GOD COULD CATCH **LIGHTNING IN A BOTTLE.**

IGOR, IT TURNED OUT, COULD **NOT.** HE TRIED CHASING IT, LURING IT . . .

HE EVEN READ IT POEMS!

ROSES ARE RED, SPARKS ARE BLUE – *GET IN THE BOTTLE!!*

IGOR BECAME A JOKE, WHICH ONLY MADE HIM MAD . . . ER MADDER.

THEY'LL ALL SEE . . . I *WILL* MASTER LIGHTNING!

AND SO HE TURNED TO THE **DARK SIDE** ...

FOUL SPIRITS FROM BEYOND SCIENCE, **HELP!!!!**

AND HIS PLEAS WERE ANSWERED.

THESE FEATHERS - THEY'RE **ALIVE WITH ELECTICITY!**

WITH HIS NEW 'PET', IGOR HAD TAMED LIGHTNING! HIS WORK WAS FINISHED.

FINISHED? OH, NO ... THEY **LAUGHED** AT ME, REMEMBER?

GET 'EM, SPARKY! NO PRISONERS!

NEXT WEEK: 'IGOR'S REVENGE!'

CHAPTER 1

A COMIC CONSPIRACY

Whippet Willow's enjoyment of the exploits of Igor McIgorvich and his electrical bird came to an untimely end when a grubby football bounced off his forehead. Whippet jumped back in surprise and dropped his comic on the floor of the bus.

'Ha! Nice header,' said Nate Rumble, turning round to address Whippet from the seat in front. 'What you going to do for your next trick, weirdo? *Draw* us a goal? Hehehe!'

Laughter exploded from the other seats. Looking up from the back row of the bus, Whippet felt a familiar hot flush of embarrassment and frustration rise in his cheeks as he gazed into a sea of grinning faces. Boys and girls from his school and from his neighbourhood. They were all looking at him and they were all laughing. Nate might have been a sad excuse for an eleven-year-old bully, but he was popular. Being good at sports seemed to make kids like you, and as Whippet knew only too well, while being laughed at by one boy wasn't particularly annoying, being laughed at by *twenty children* was just horrible.

Unless, that is, you knew how to play the game.

Whippet lifted the football from his lap and stared at it. Then he pulled a pencil from his pocket. He looked up at Nate and smiled.

'You know actually Nate, I think I'd much rather draw a tiny little hole,' said Whippet.

Nate frowned.

'What's this nutter talking about?' he said, turning round to address the rest of the bus.

Whippet gave his pencil a wiggle then tapped it, point down, on the top of the football.

'Isn't it obvious?

I'm going to draw a hole, right here. Right on the side of your precious ball. But it's difficult drawing on leather so I might have to push quite *hard*.'

Nate swallowed hard. The tip of Whippet's pencil looked freshly sharpened. Nate's confidence wavered. Everyone knew Whippet was a bit strange, but surely he wouldn't go that far? Surely he could take a joke? *Surely!*

The others craned over the backs of their seats to see what would happen.

'I was just kidding, Whippet! Don't do anything silly,' said Nate, his eyes growing wider and wider with concern.

Whippet gave his pencil one more waggle, enjoying the way Nate's whole body flinched in fear. Then he shook his head and tossed the ball back. Nate caught it and hurriedly dropped back into his seat. The fun was clearly over, so everyone else copied him.

Everyone except for Danica Patel. The pretty girl with brown eyes and hair as black as Whippet's own unruly mop had not laughed when Nate threw the ball. She had frowned. But Whippet hadn't seen Danica's reaction as he was too busy retrieving his comic from the footwell.

Whippet opened the zipper on the rucksack at his feet and swapped his copy of last week's **FREAKY** for his travel sketch-book. He flicked slowly through the pages, critiquing his recent scribbles, checking them for mistakes or looking for improvements. When it came to drawing he was a bit of a perfectionist.

'What a loony,' said Nate to the rest of the bus. 'You know, I heard he actually eats pencils. For breakfast.'

'It was ONE pencil, alright,' shouted Whippet, before adding, 'And I ate it before dinner!'

He turned to the boy sitting beside him.

'Mossy, how's it the holidays and yet we're still spending time with this lot?'

Simon Moss, Whippet's best friend in the whole world, looked up from his phone in confusion.

'Sorry, buddy, what did you say?'

'Nothing. Forget it. Hey, where did you get that?' said Whippet.

Simon held up his mobile phone.

'After our last crazy adventure, Mum decided it might be time for me to have a phone of my own. She didn't like Ruby and me coming home so late. So the phone's for, you know, emergencies and stuff.'

Whippet raised his eyebrows, then looked around to see if anyone was listening. When he was satisfied, he leaned in closer to whisper.

'Emergencies, eh? That's cool, Mossy, really cool. But answer me this: who are you going to call if we run into another nose-stealing, rubbish-collecting, sister-kidnapping, truck-sized *MONSTER?* The army? The police? The zoo? Your *dad?*'

Simon stared at his hysterical friend and nodded thoughtfully. Whippet was extremely prone to flights of fancy surrounding daft conspiracy theories. He had a bad habit of thinking the world was out to get him. Personally.

It was usually harmless nonsense, but not in this case. In this case he had a very good point.

It had been two weeks since the boys had battled to rescue Simon's younger sister, Ruby, from the clutches of a monstrous beast known as the

Snotticus Galavantia. The Snotticus had been
a truly bizarre creature, and it had made a
strange lair for itself in the sewers beneath
their home town of Lake Shore. In the end
they'd defeated it through a combination of
dumb luck, good fortune and the help of a
terrifyingly fearless nine-year-old girl.

Simon shuddered thinking about it.
The memory of the encounter was so vivid
it seemed like yesterday.

Whippet turned away from his friend

and gazed out of the window. He let out a
long sigh that misted the glass. Drawing in
the steam with his finger, he slowly sketched
a picture of a skull with a frown, which
perfectly matched his own expression.

'I like things a little freaky, Mossy, you
know that, but I think this trip is a bad idea.
We're heading for trouble, buddy. T-R-O-
U-B-L-E. The forces of darkness are
gathering. They've always had our number
and now they're coming for us . . . I can
feel it in my bones.'

Another laugh rose from the seat in

front. Whippet's wild theories had never been taken seriously by his fellow students. He shook his head and stared at his now dripping picture of a skull, the condensation having started to run down the glass.

'I agree,' said Simon in a whisper. 'There's something really weird going on, but we've been hiding at home for a fortnight. We had to get out or people would begin to ask some difficult questions. Mum was already starting to wonder why I'd stopped playing outside. We *needed* this Explorers' camping trip. You don't want to be scared forever, do you?'

'No,' said Whippet, 'but hiding is a fine way of dealing with problems. See, there are plenty of reasons why I don't leave my home, and the threat of a surprise monster attack, while spending a weekend with a bunch of total morons, is TOP of my list.'

Simon, like most children, usually looked forward to escaping the confines of his home and adventuring far from the prying eyes of his parents. But Whippet Willow was NOT most children. He had two main interests – drawing comics and reading comics. His favourite comic of all time being the gore-filled shock-fest known as **FREAKY**. Whippet liked to practise both of these pastimes indoors. With the curtains drawn. And his bedroom door securely locked, bolted and chained.

Whippet's mum had other ideas however, and was rather keen that her son learned how to 'play nicely with others'. Which is how Whippet came to find himself on the bus with Simon, bound for the annual Lake Shore Explorers' Camp, for the first time in his life. Simon was a veteran of the camp, having made the journey every summer since he was eight years old.

'You're going to love this place, pal. And it's all about safety in numbers,' said Simon, punching Whippet lightly on the arm in a cheerful manner. 'Nothing's going to happen if we stick together. There won't be any beasties waiting to pounce on us from the bushes. And we definitely won't run into any psychotic nine-year-old girls carrying bazookas.'

Simon hated to admit it, but he was actually a little sad about the second point. Lucy Shufflebottom, the bazooka-carrying girl in question, was certainly dangerous, but she really had been the key to rescuing Ruby from the Snotticus. Lucy knew how to fire a crossbow without shooting yourself in the foot, and a lot more besides. She was resourceful and clever and she seemed to be terrifyingly comfortable in the presence of monsters. He wished he had some way of contacting her, but he had no idea where she lived, or even where she went to school.

Simon leaned back in his chair and scratched his chin. Without Lucy's help he and Whippet would have been lost in the sewers. Dead lost. Or just dead. *Perhaps Whippet is right to be worried*, thought Simon. The boys had discussed endless theories about the origins of the Snotticus over the

past fortnight but they had learned nothing. They'd tried to research the beast on the internet but they couldn't find a single mention of it. Lake Shore's library had a good collection of wildlife books but there was nothing that looked even slightly like their monster. Everywhere they turned they'd drawn a blank.

It was all a big weird mystery, and one that Simon's dad had been extremely interested to hear about. At the start of the summer, he had left home to work abroad on some big project for the government. At least, that was what Simon remembered him saying, but he hadn't paid much attention to the details at the time. It had sounded pretty scientific and Simon was hopeless at science.

But before Dad left on his travels, he had made it clear to Simon that he wanted to hear if anything odd happened in the town of Lake Shore. A sister-kidnapping monster definitely counted as ODD in Simon's book, so he'd shared the tale of their adventure.

Strangely for a grown-up, instead of thinking his son had made it all up, Simon's dad merely asked him more questions.

Lots of questions.

How many nostrils did it have? How fast could it run? Did Simon touch it? What did it feel like? What did it sound like? What colour was it? Questions and questions and questions.

Well, thought Simon, his fingers returning to the keypad and the unfinished email on his phone, *I've answered your questions and now I've got one of my own.*

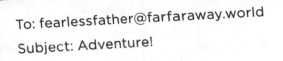

To: fearlessfather@farfaraway.world

Subject: Adventure!

Hey Dad,

Whippet and I are off to the Explorers' Camp for the weekend. It should be pretty cool as it's in Wailing Wood, which is home to more unique species of bird than anywhere else in the world. Better yet, there's a rumour that the forest is supposed to be haunted! I don't really believe in ghosts but after what happened with the Snotticus, I'm not so sure about anything any more. I will certainly be keeping my eyes open for anything weird

I want to ask you something, Dad, and it's going to sound a bit silly. What is it, exactly, that you do at work? I know I've not been all that interested in your job before but that was before. Everything feels different now. It's weird not knowing what you're doing when you're away for so long.

Anyway, I'd really like to know. Oh, and this will be my last email for a couple of days. Mr Recks, our camp leader, said our phones won't work in the woods. Bad signal or something.

Worst news still – worst news EVER, actually – I won't have any new comic stories from *Freaky* or *Fearless* to share with you this week! We had to get on the bus so early this morning that the shops weren't even open. Whippet thinks it's some sort of comic conspiracy and I agree!

Still, we'll try to survive without them . . . but it is going to be HARD.

Mum and Ruby miss you loads. And I miss you too.

Bye for now!

Simon

Simon hit send. He stared at the screen and thought about the one detail he *hadn't* shared with his father, the one detail from their encounter with the Snotticus that both he and Whippet had really struggled to understand.

His storytelling superpower.

Twice during that adventure, when Simon had found himself backed into a corner, he'd discovered that he could hypnotise both his friends and a giant monster just by telling a tall tale. He had stopped them all in their tracks with the power of a good story.

It made as little sense as the Snotticus itself, but somehow Simon couldn't bring himself to tell his dad about it. The ability scared him a bit, and now he was actually beginning to doubt if it had even worked in the first place. Since they got back he'd tried to practise it on his sister Ruby but had failed miserably. She'd just laughed at his very best stories, before scampering off to turn the house upside down. Not literally, but pretty literally.

It was all a bit embarrassing, and Simon had decided to stop telling stories for a while until he could work out what he was doing wrong.

The bus had slowed to a halt. Simon looked up as the engine was switched off. The bus fell silent.

'What? Are we there already? That was quick,' said Simon in surprise.

Whippet pressed his face up against the

window. He looked left and right, then spun back round. Simon laughed at the large condensation drip that was hanging from his friend's nose. Whippet shook his head with a grin to loosen the droplet. His eyes were wide and his smile was genuine. He looked excited. Extremely excited.

'Mossy, you are not going to *believe* where we've stopped!'

And Whippet was right.

CHAPTER 2

THE PIRATE
AND THE T-REX

Rising from their seats, Simon, Whippet and the others filed slowly off the bus and joined their camp leader, who was standing on the pavement outside a very familiar shop.

Mr Recks, or Ted Recks to use his full

name – or 'T-Rex', as the kids liked to call him – was a towering figure. Over seven feet tall and bulging with muscles, T-Rex looked as if he'd stepped from the pages of a fantasy comic. Whippet often described him as Frankenstein's monster's *big brother*, but this comparison was not quite accurate. As far as Simon was concerned, T-Rex looked and sounded exactly like a caveman.

'Bus stop. Need supplies,' barked T-Rex, with a voice like a stone axe beating on a drum made from baked triceratops hide. 'Kids want comics?'

The camp master pointed a giant thumb over his shoulder at the building behind him. Every child nodded frantically, grinning as they stared up at the town's famous Shipshape Shop. As the name suggested, the shop was actually a huge old Spanish galleon, complete with masts and barnacles and cannon, and was home to countless comics, toys and basically all manner of good stuff.

Simon couldn't believe what he was hearing. He raised his hand.

'T-Rex . . . I mean *Mr* Recks,' said Simon, hurriedly choking back the camp master's nickname. 'Er, the Shipshape Shop doesn't open for two hours. Captain

Armstrong *never* opens early. Never ever. Ever.'

T-Rex laughed. It was a big laugh.

'T-Rex good name. Me keep. But Simon wrong. Shop open for T-Rex.'

As if on cue, the double front doors of the shop swung slowly outwards. Twenty-two pairs of young eyes gazed in amazement as, striding into the early-morning light, the ever-impressive figure of Captain Armstrong appeared.

The Captain stopped in the middle of the pavement, placed his hands on his hips and breathed deeply, his eyes shut. Then he exhaled with a long, slow whistle.

'Aar, smell that fresh air. It be good to blow the barnacles from me beard and the woodworm from me wooden leg,' he said.

Captain Armstrong was a gnarly old sea dog to be sure. At least, that was how he

appeared. He spoke like a pirate and dressed like a Royal Naval officer from the eighteenth century, but this was generally considered by the adults of Lake Shore to be nothing more than a cunning way to sell comics and toys and sweets. You couldn't fake a wooden leg, though (Whippet had tried) and Lucy had been pretty convincing when she'd told the boys that Captain

Armstrong actually was, really, seriously, a pirate.

Still, it was a bit of a leap of faith, but Simon didn't care. The Captain was cool.

T-Rex thumped his fist against his chest. One big thump. Captain Armstrong raised an eyebrow at the camp leader, then gave a small nod. It was a reaction so subtle that most people would have missed it, but not Simon. Not any more. After their fight with the Snotticus, Simon had started paying close attention to the details of their weird town and in particular the actions of Captain Armstrong. Lucy had hinted that the Captain was a part of a bigger mystery and Simon was keen to find out what he knew.

Captain Armstrong spread his arms in greeting.

'Kids, today I be breakin' all the rules!

My store be *yours* to browse in private! Ye will be the very first to lay your 'ands on today's fresh comic booty.'

There was a cheer from the group and they hurriedly pulled out their wallets and purses.

Captain Armstrong held up his palms to calm the crowd.

'I'll be in to plunder your doubloons shortly . . . but first I've a little *errand* to attend to,' said the Captain.

Everyone rushed forwards, piling through the doors to grab their precious comics and stock up on sweet treats for the weekend. Simon and Whippet had been sitting at the back of the bus, so were last off and found themselves at the rear of the group waiting to enter the shop.

'You like comics, don't you, Whippet?' said a soft voice from beside them.

The boys spun in surprise to find Danica standing beside them.

'Er, yep. Yeah. I like comics. Yes. I do,' said Whippet, and then, because he felt it only polite to throw something back, he asked, 'Do . . . do you like comics?'

'Sure, but I prefer detective stories. You know, following the clues, doggedly hunting your prey . . . finally getting your man.'

Danica gave a brief smile and then strolled away without a backwards glance,

leaving Whippet and Simon all alone in the street, which was how Simon came to notice the Captain sidle quietly up to T-Rex and whisper a brief, mysterious exchange.

'You an' I need to parlay, T-Rex. *The Den*. Right now!'

'But who mind shop?' replied T-Rex.

'Oh, it'll look after itself for a minute or two. But *this* won't keep . . .'

Simon resisted the urge to look at either the pirate or the caveman. Instead he acted casual and followed his best friend inside the shop. Once out of sight from the others, he dragged Whippet into a dark corner nook of the store, hidden from view. All around them sagging shelves weighed down by mountains of art supplies threatened to collapse and crush them to death.

'What are you doing, Mossy? And what was up with Danica?' began Whippet, but then his eyes took in their surroundings. He gazed in wonder at the pencils, paints, crayons, paper, sketchbooks and card that filled every inch of the space.

'Oh, wow . . . thanks for the reminder! I was down to my last pencil and if I'd blunted it on Nate's football I'd have been in *real* trouble.'

'Sorry, we're not here for pencils,' said Simon. 'Something is going on. And by something, I mean *something freaky.*'

Simon removed a large stack of crêpe paper from a shelf in order to make a space through which the boys could observe the rest of the shop.

'Nice spy hole, Mossy. But what are we

spying on?' asked Whippet, peering over his friend's shoulder.

'Those two,' said Simon.

In the far corner of the shop, away from the piled comics that were currently captivating the interests of the other kids, Captain Armstrong and T-Rex were standing in front of another T-Rex. It was a ten-foot-tall display case, shaped exactly like a dinosaur. The creature's head was bent low and a number of shelves had been built into its vast open mouth, each holding a range of prehistoric action figures.

As Simon and Whippet watched in amazement, the dinosaur silently raised its large head, revealing a hidden opening in the wall. Captain Armstrong and T-Rex

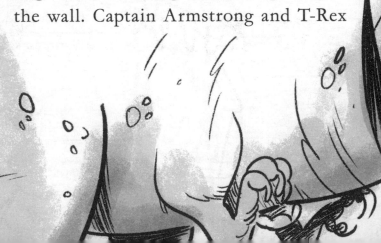

quickly crept inside, letting the head fell back into place.

They had disappeared.

Simon looked at Whippet. Whippet looked at Simon. Neither boy could keep the smile from his face.

'A secret door,' they whispered in unison, before sneaking round the shelves to approach the T-Rex.

Whippet shook his head slowly in disbelief as Simon peered into the mouth of the beast.

'Just when you think the Shipshape Shop can't get any cooler, you discover Captain Armstrong keeps a trapdoor inside a dinosaur! Beat that,' grinned Whippet.

'No time for admiration, Whippet. Give me a hand,' said Simon. 'I don't know what they pressed but there has to be a hidden switch here somewhere. If we're going to get in there we have to find it.'

Whippet ran his hands over the figures on the shelves, picking them up at random while Simon tested every one of the dinosaur's teeth. Sixty is a lot of teeth and by the time he'd finished, and found nothing, he had started to despair. To make matters more annoying, Whippet seemed to have lost interest a while ago and was just standing and staring at the T-Rex.

'Great. Thanks for the help, pal,' said Simon sarcastically.

'What do you know about Captain Armstrong?' said Whippet, without turning his gaze from the dinosaur.

'Well, let's see. He thinks he's a pirate. He *might* be a pirate.'

'What else?'

'Er, he likes to tell tales. Tales of his legendary battles with giant beasts on the high seas.'

'He certainly does. Now, think carefully. How does Captain Armstrong actually *beat* most of those monsters?'

Simon scratched his head.

'Well, by *staring* at them. He challenged most of them to staring contests . . . if what he says is true.'

Whippet nodded.

'Exactly. As far as Captain Armstrong's concerned, if you want to get past a beastie you have to look them right in the *EYE*.'

Then, as Simon watched, Whippet stretched upwards and poked the T-Rex in the left eyeball. The eye moved backwards under his touch with a soft *click*.

There was a faint whirring sound then the dinosaur raised its head once more. Through the hole in the wall the boys could see a narrow wood-panelled passage.

'Brilliant,' said Simon, bumping knuckles with Whippet. 'Absolutely brilliant!'

Whippet grinned and gave an elaborate bow, then gestured to the entrance.

'After you, Mossy.'

The two boys crept inside, filled with a mixture of excitement and fear.

CHAPTER 3

SECRETS AND SPIES

As they moved along the corridor, Simon held a finger to his lips for radio silence and Whippet nodded. The boys were experienced spies.

Long before their adventure with the Snotticus, Simon and Whippet had begun practising the art of effective sneaking and peeking, and they'd put it to good use. Their skills had helped them discover where Whippet's mum kept her secret stash of chocolate biscuits, where Simon's dad had kept the keys to the shed (in which they found all manner of dangerous tools with which to mess around) and even who was posting cards in the school Valentine's box.

This last one was especially important. If there was one thing which the boys shared *more* than their mutual love of comics, it was their mutual suspicion of girls. While they accepted that Lucy Shufflebottom was a bit of an exception, it was only because she was a dangerous lunatic. Danica, on the other hand, well, who knew *what* went on in her head.

Creeping to the end of the corridor, the boys found themselves at the top of a ladder. The only option was downwards. Simon led the way. Stepping from the last rung, he felt the floor beneath his feet give a slight creak. The boys were in a vast, dingy storeroom, the only light provided by a few flickering oil lamps hung from the wall. The space looked to be roughly the same size as the entire Shipshape Shop above. Packing boxes, crates and ancient chests were stacked in wonky piles, covered in faded and peeling labels and secured with frayed rope. Whippet sniffed the air then screwed up his nose.

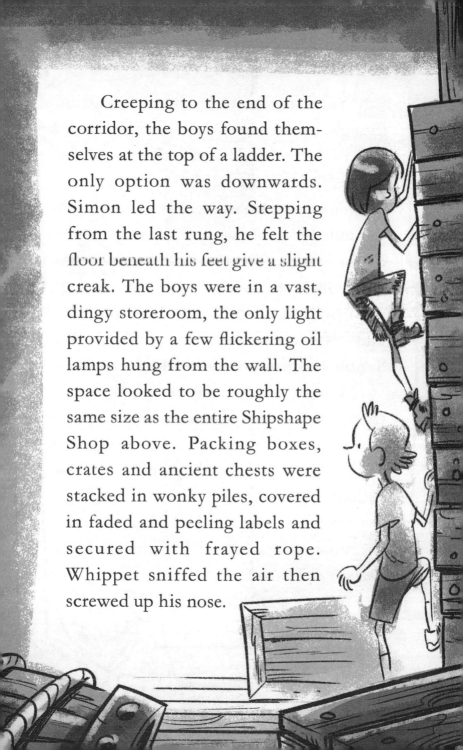

'Yikes, no wonder Captain Armstrong thought the air smelled fresh outside. Get a whiff of this place! It stinks like old fish stewing in a mouldy sock.'

Simon breathed in. The strong scent reminded him of last year's family holiday to the seaside. The breeze from the ocean had blown the smell of the sea through their bedroom window each night. Ruby had complained about it constantly, but Simon had grown to quite like it.

'The more I see and smell, Whippet, the more I start to believe that Captain Armstrong really is a pirate. Just look at this place. We could be standing inside an actual galleon.'

He bent down and picked at a label on the nearest tea chest. It read *Cutlasses, Daggers and Dirks.*

'What's a Dirk?' whispered Whippet.

'No idea . . . a dork crossed with a jerk, perhaps,' said Simon with a grin.

Whippet fought to swallow his laughter, desperately trying not to make a noise, which set Simon off.

'Let's go find T-Rex and the Captain,' he chuckled, after they'd got control of their giggles.

Scurrying through the maze of crates, they suddenly heard their camp leader's distinctive booming voice. It was coming from a grand doorway at the end of the storeroom. The door was ajar and warm light was spilling through the gap. Simon and Whippet crawled closer and pressed themselves up against the frame. Through the open door the boys could see Captain Armstrong slumped in a wooden armchair. Well, it was more like a throne. There were flintlock pistols and rubies and weird hooks

embedded in the woodwork and what looked like a giant monkey's skull mounted on the top. As chairs went, it was pretty spectacular.

The Captain sat on his throne behind a chipped and scarred wooden desk, against which T-Rex was leaning. The table seemed to be buckling slightly under his immense bulk.

'Me not see problem,' said T-Rex. 'Time they learn to defend themselves. Be all they can be.'

'Well, you would say that, because you be a *grunt*. Best o' the best, no doubt, but ye be a foot soldier. Infantry. They send you to do the dirty work. The 'eavy lifting, NOT the 'eavy *thinking*.'

T-Rex cracked his knuckles. It sounded like a dozen coconuts being shattered, which was weird as he only had ten fingers like everyone else.

'T-Rex like dirty work. Find enemy. Crush enemy. Go home. Drink tea. Sleep well.'

'Listen, take it from a scurvy sea dog who knows what 'e's talkin' about: this one feels different. I don't think they're ready for what be out there.'

Simon froze. Who were they talking about?

Captain Armstrong continued.

'Yes, I read the report from Knuckles, an' although 'e didn't see the battle 'imself, it sounds like the three kids did a remarkable job. Ran into ol' nosey once myself, back in the day. Nasty thing. Defeating that beast was impressive stuff for a first encounter, an' if the rumour that one of the lads is a TELLER turns out to be true, well . . . there be no knowin' *what* they'll be capable of in the future.'

Whippet looked across the doorway at his friend and mouthed the words *Knuckles* and *Teller*. Simon shrugged. It was all very confusing. Were they talking about their encounter with the Snotticus? If so, that would mean that this mysterious-sounding 'Teller' must be one of them.

'Me still not see problem,' said T-Rex.

'The problem is that their future not be *NOW*. This trip be too risky. Seems like something foul is escaping every other week. You and I are going to need to have a word with the men upstairs. Take the latest beastie. It be dangerous. Real dangerous. I tell you, the forces of darkness be gatherin'. They've always 'ad our number an' now they're comin' for us . . . I can feel it in me bones. An' me leg. My real leg.'

Simon looked across the doorway at his friend. It was Whippet's turn to shake his head and shrug. The Captain's last words echoed Whippet's own paranoid theory from the bus, almost word for word.

'T-Rex find danger. Kids stay safe. T-Rex protect them. T-Rex *Guardian*,' said the camp leader, waving a huge wooden club over his head. Simon hadn't seen him pull it out, and had no idea where he'd been hiding the great big stick. The club was taller than Simon.

Captain Armstrong sighed.

'Aye, you are. An' as Guardians, all THREE of us – you, me and Knuckles – we all signed the Treaty, remember? We observe. We report. We act as the last line of *defence*, not attack,' said the Captain. 'We don't start the fightin' any more, an' we're only allowed to step in when things get *really* out of 'and. Times be bad, I grant ye, but they not be out of 'and. Not yet, anyway.'

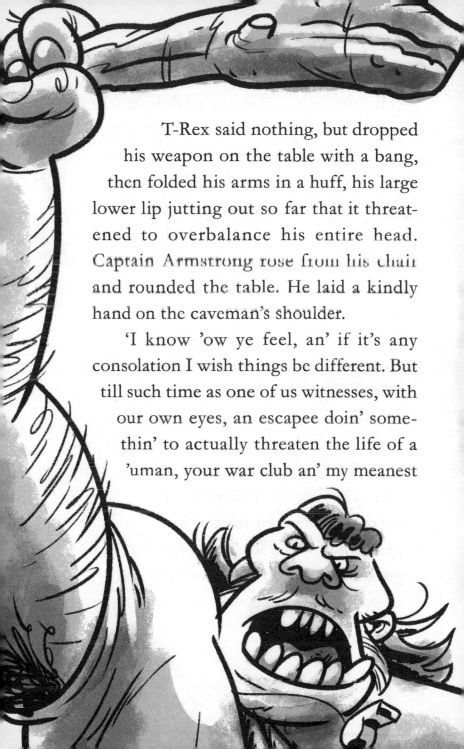

T-Rex said nothing, but dropped his weapon on the table with a bang, then folded his arms in a huff, his large lower lip jutting out so far that it threatened to overbalance his entire head. Captain Armstrong rose from his chair and rounded the table. He laid a kindly hand on the caveman's shoulder.

'I know 'ow ye feel, an' if it's any consolation I wish things be different. But till such time as one of us witnesses, with our own eyes, an escapee doin' somethin' to actually threaten the life of a 'uman, your war club an' my meanest *stare* will 'ave to stay 'olstered. Rule number one, remember? We don't blow our cover. Our true identity must remain a secret.'

T-Rex raised one massive eyebrow.

'But . . . but if T-Rex *see* beast, T-Rex can *stop* it?'

'With gusto. Otherwise those kids be on their own. Keep them in your sight and there should be no reason to worry. But mark my words, trouble's waiting in those woods. It knows you're coming. I just 'ope the kids are prepared for the unexpected . . . I 'ope they'll be keeping their eyes wide open . . . an' I REALLY 'ope they learn 'ow to work together,' he said with a grave look.

The room fell quiet.

The conversation was at an end.

Simon tilted his head towards the store-room and Whippet took the hint. The boys crept away in silence, lost in their own thoughts and fears. Slowly they wormed their way back through the heaped fish-scented boxes and crates, back to the ladder, back up through the dinosaur, and out into the Shipshape Shop where happy kids bustled around with their new comics. Simon and Whippet were focused on the same thing: the promise of an unknown danger waiting for them down the road, something serious enough to worry a caveman and a pirate. What neither boy saw as they made their escape was the caveman and the pirate staring at the doorway where they'd just been hiding.

Captain Armstrong nodded to himself, his mouth curved into a small, sad smile.

'And THAT be all we can do for 'em, T-Rex – without breaking the rules. Good luck, me 'earties.'

CHAPTER 4

THE LIMOUSINE KID

Simon and Whippet hung around at the back of the shop as the rest of the group made their purchases. Captain Armstrong had not re-emerged through the dinosaur passage. Instead he had popped up behind the counter, as if by magic. Simon guessed there had to be another exit. Just how many mysteries could one Shipshape Shop contain?

'It's no good, Mossy, I can't buy anything. I'm hopeless at fibbing. He'll see it in my eyes. He'll ask me what's up and I'll tell him, "Everything! *Everything!*"' said Whippet miserably.

Simon nodded. Even before he'd discovered his strange power, Simon had been a fantastic storyteller, capable of making up weird and wonderful tales on the spot. But stories were one thing; LIES were something very different. Lies had a nasty habit of coming undone at exactly the wrong moment, like a pair of trousers falling down in the middle of the playground.

Simon shuddered at the thought. No one liked to be caught with their pants down. And besides, a week without comics wasn't the worst thing to happen to the boys recently. Not by a long way.

Whippet and Simon left the shop and headed for the bus, where another surprise lay in wait. T-Rex was already sitting in the driver's seat.

'All done?' boomed the camp leader, frowning at the boys' empty hands and wide eyes.

'Yep, uh-huh,' said Whippet, hurriedly climbing on to the bus and shuffling up the aisle towards their seats at the back, his head bowed the whole way.

Simon paused beside T-Rex. He felt they owed their camp leader more of an explanation. Missing out on the weekly comics was still a pretty big deal in Lake Shore.

'We, er, forgot to bring any money,' said Simon with a wonky grin.

'Then this lucky day,' said T-Rex, reaching down to extract an envelope from beside his seat. He passed it to Simon, who stared at it in confusion.

'Captain say you two no miss out.'

T-Rex turned away to stare out of the windscreen and Simon took that as a sign that their little talk was over. He headed up the bus, flopped down next to Whippet and upended the envelope over his friend's lap. Mint-condition copies of the latest issues of **FREAKY** and **FEARLESS** fell into Whippet's open palms. Whippet stared at the comics in wonder.

'Where did you —' he began, but he was interrupted as the bus exploded with noise. The others were piling back onboard.

'We'll talk about it *all* later,' said Simon, 'when we reach the camp.'

As soon as everyone was settled, T-Rex pulled away from the kerb and left the Shipshape Shop behind. The bus wound slowly through the streets and on to Turnaway Bridge, with its strange collection of stone gargoyles hidden underneath. Once upon a time the bridge had scared Simon in such an unexplainable way that he'd had to screw his eyes shut to avoid even looking at it — and when he and Whippet and Lucy had tracked the Snotticus to the bridge, his fears hadn't seemed quite so unfounded after all. Beating that monster might have helped Simon conquer his fear of Turnaway Bridge but it had also given him new horrors to worry about. He had no idea where the Snotticus had come from or why it had lured him to its lair. How could he prepare himself for another attack if he didn't have a clue about his enemy?

Over the lake they drove and on through the quiet morning streets. Passing the last row of houses, they left the narrow lanes behind and sped up. Moments later, the familiar town sign flew past – *NOW LEAVING LAKE SHORE! HAVE A NICE DAY?*

Simon did a double-take. The sign had been there forever, the words painted on a big piece of shiny triangular metal that had been stuck in the ground. He'd seen it so many times and yet he'd never really *looked* at it. It was just a big shiny sign. But, as with everything else in town, Simon was now looking with fresh eyes. Looking for clues.

The metal sign was actually the wing of a *plane*. A fighter plane too, complete with mounted cannon!

Simon shook his head in disbelief. Then another thought occurred to him. The message itself, *HAVE A NICE DAY?* Why had someone painted a question mark on the end? Would today be a nice day? If Captain Armstrong was right, then probably *not*.

Simon knew he had every reason to be worried, but as the strange sign and the town of Lake Shore receded into the distance, his heart

NOW LEAVING LAKE SHORE!

HAVE A NICE DAY?

began to lighten. They were off on a trip, he had a new comic in his hand, and T-Rex was a reassuring presence in the bus. And the further he drove them from town, the better Simon felt. Perhaps everything would be okay. Perhaps today would be fun.

It seemed that Whippet did not share his optimistic outlook. He'd bitten his nails so low that he'd actually run out of nail and had started on the fingers. Simon kicked his feet up against the seat in front and put his hands behind his head, trying to look as relaxed as possible.

'How about, just for today, we forget the Captain and T-Rex's strange conversation? We don't really know who they were talking about. Anyway, we're being led by a caveman on an adventure! This is about as safe a place as we could find. *Nothing* exciting is going to happen to us.'

'I seem to remember saying something similar the other week,' said Whippet.

'Good point, my friend. But lightning doesn't strike twice,' said Simon. He instantly regretted the comment.

BANG! BANG!

The bus shook with the sound of two loud **BANG!**s. Two ALMIGHTY **BANG!**s. Simon, Whippet and the other kids suddenly found themselves catapulted into the air as, with a terrifying squeal, the bus ground to a violent halt. Half a second later they returned to earth, landing in a heap at the front of the bus.

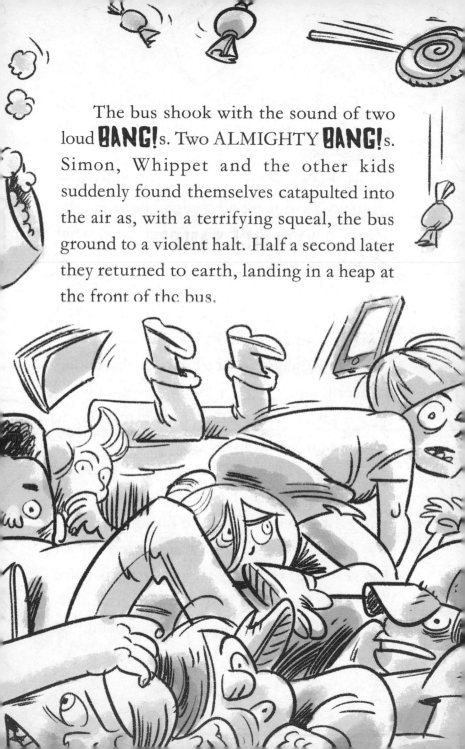

Comics and sweets rained down on their heads as they struggled to untangle themselves.

'I don't want to nitpick,' said Whippet, lying upside down and wedged between the seats, 'but if THAT wasn't exciting, what would you call it?'

T-Rex turned from the steering wheel and stared at the pile of kids. He looked worried and annoyed in equal measure.

'Kids okay? No one hurt?' he barked in concern.

'Ugh . . . I think I broke my funny bone,' said Whippet.

'However will you survive without *that*?' said Nate Rumble sarcastically, struggling to rise from the bundle of kids.

It was a mess. T-Rex squeezed out of his seat and, reaching down with his giant mitts, he began to help separate the chil-dren, lifting them up like they weighed nothing at all.

'T-Rex brake. This bad. Flying kids not make parents happy.'

Simon had to agree with that one. His mum still worried when he walked into town on his own.

'It not matter. We here. Everyone up. Grab bags. Off bus,' he said and – with a tiny blink-and-you'd-miss-it grin at Simon and Whippet – the camp leader shouldered his way back down the narrow aisle and out through the front door.

'Was that a SMILE? What's he *smiling* about?' whispered Whippet, still struggling to right himself. An outstretched hand dropped into his view and he grabbed it gratefully. Whippet was pulled upright.

Brushing himself down, Whippet breathed a sigh of relief.

'Cheers, Mossy, I thought I'd never get – oh.'

Simon was lying on the floor by his feet. Whippet looked up. His helping hand actually belonged to Danica. She really was a very pretty girl, thought Whippet, being uncharacteristically honest with himself. She was studying him again with big, brown, serious eyes.

'Sorry about that! Thanks, Danica,' said Whippet.

Danica's mouth turned up slowly at the edges. It could have been a smile or a smirk

– it was hard to tell.

'You really must learn to stand up for yourself, Whippet,' she said.

Then Danica turned and walked away.

Whippet's mouth opened. Then closed. He grabbed Simon and helped him up.

'Well, that's becoming an odd habit . . .' said Simon, watching Danica hop down the steps and off the bus.

'Be sure to let me know when something odd *doesn't* happen,' said Whippet as they grabbed their bags and jumped off the bus to join the others. The weather had turned during the drive and a light drizzle had begun to fall. T-Rex didn't seem to mind.

'Welcome to Lake Shore Explorers' Camp,' he bellowed with a genuine smile.

The group found themselves standing beneath a wooden archway constructed

over a rough gravel pathway. The path sloped away, gently downwards towards the distant woodland. It was lined along both sides with large irregular-sized rocks. Nailed to the top of the framework above them was the campsite's name, each letter made from thick branches that had been tied together with rope.

'Wailing Wood home to many birds. More birds than anywhere in world. Woods are twitcher paradise!' said T-Rex.

Whippet frowned.

'What's a *twitcher?* Is it like some sort of government agent? Do they watch twits? Like us?' he whispered to Simon,

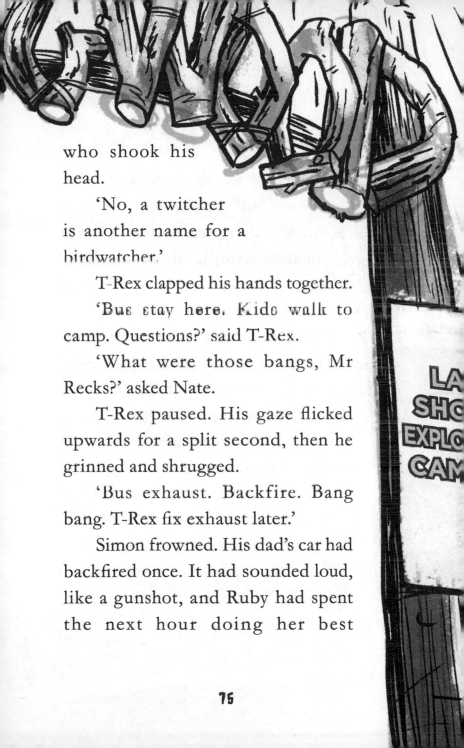

who shook his
head.

'No, a twitcher
is another name for a
birdwatcher.'

T-Rex clapped his hands together.

'Bus stay here. Kids walk to
camp. Questions?' said T-Rex.

'What were those bangs, Mr
Recks?' asked Nate.

T-Rex paused. His gaze flicked
upwards for a split second, then he
grinned and shrugged.

'Bus exhaust. Backfire. Bang
bang. T-Rex fix exhaust later.'

Simon frowned. His dad's car had
backfired once. It had sounded loud,
like a gunshot, and Ruby had spent
the next hour doing her best

impression of the noise, which Simon had found rather funny, and his parents had most definitely not.

But that wasn't the sound he'd heard on the bus. There had been a charge to the noise. A spark. An edge. Whippet gave him a nudge, and his friend nodded towards the road in front of the bus. Two circular black marks had been scorched into the surface. Both were smoking slightly, wisps of steam rising and hissing as the light rain continued to fall.

"'Lightning doesn't strike twice'?" whispered Whippet, and Simon's eyes expanded in surprise.

'Two lightning strikes, that close together? Wow . . . I guess it's our lucky day,' said Simon in relief.

Before Whippet could challenge Simon's idea of 'lucky', the air was filled with a more tuneful interruption: a musical blast from a car horn. Everyone stared up the lane, where the longest, blackest, sleekest car they had ever seen was parked on the grass verge.

'Ah, T-Rex forget,' said their camp leader, slapping his huge forehead. 'New boy join. First camping trip. Play nice.'

As they watched, the furthest, furthest, *furthest* car door slowly opened and out stepped a small boy. Tiny, in fact. He was dragging a simply huge holdall behind him. It was as long as a coffin. To make matters more ridiculous the boy was wearing a base-ball cap that was probably made to fit an

adult, because it fell right over his face, hiding everything except his mouth. And that mouth was curled into an expression of *extreme* annoyance.

'Er, hello. What's your name?' asked Simon, holding out his hand as the boy approached the group. It was a bit of a formal gesture, but the boy had arrived in a limousine, after all. His family must be rich and important. Shaking hands was probably something he did a lot.

The boy walked towards Simon's outstretched open palm. Then, at the last possible moment, he stepped to the side, zigzagged around Simon, and headed straight for T-Rex, his great bag in tow.

The boy handed the camp leader a piece

of paper. T-Rex traced the words on the page with his massive index finger, then shook his head in pain at the effort of reading and passed the note to Danica. The girl coughed once then spoke aloud. Whippet was surprised to find himself thinking that even her voice was pretty.

'*To Whom It May Concern. My name is Joe Bloggs. I cannot speak because I have lost my voice. Probably because of some rare and exotic disease which has the entire scientific community baffled.*

I hope one day we can all be great friends but until then, if you value your life, leave me alone.'

Joe Bloggs gave a little wave, but it wasn't aimed at the group. Instead it was

the limousine driver who waved back, then the car slowly drove away into the misty drizzle.

'Right, good. All here. Now find camp!' said T-Rex, and set off up the path.

The rest of the kids followed their camp leader. The rain was getting stronger but no one really cared. Joe Bloggs paused for a moment, his head swivelling to one side to stare at the two black marks on the road. Then he trotted after the group, his bag scraping along the ground as he went.

Whippet fell into step beside Simon.

'That Joe . . . his note . . . what a weirdo. He totally ignored you!'

'Be nice, Whippet,' said Danica, over her shoulder. 'Weirdoes stick together.'

Whippet scowled to himself while Simon considered Joe Bloggs. He did seem a bit strange, but then again, who wasn't?

'You know, Danica's got a point,' said

Simon. 'Us weirdoes should stick together. Plus, it might be his first trip away from home. Maybe he's only here because his parents had to go away somewhere else. Being left behind is almost as bad as leaving home yourself.'

This was as close as Simon had come to admitting that he really, *really* missed his dad.

'Okay, fine. Whatever,' said Whippet, entirely missing the point of Simon's observation. Then all of a sudden he stopped walking and let out a gasp of delight.

'Weirdo or not, I think I know why he wanted to come along. Look! This place is so cool! I didn't realise I was signing up for a weekend at *CAMP CREEPY!*'

They'd reached the end of the short path. As he drew up beside his friend Simon realised what Whippet was talking about.

The camp was one giant freaky mess.

CHAPTER 5

CAMP CREEPY

T-Rex slowed and the group stopped dead
in their tracks. Everyone stared at the
campsite.

'Hmm . . . this place seen better days,'
said T-Rex, scratching his huge chin.

This is what is known in grown-up
conversation as an *understatement*.

What T-Rex really meant was that the

camp should be demolished and rebuilt, as it was a wreck and possibly quite dangerous. Correction. Not 'quite dangerous', but a death-trap. Judging from their surroundings, they'd walked into the middle of a bombsite.

Four wooden cabins sat near the edge of Wailing Wood. They were arranged around a central clearing like spokes on a bicycle wheel. A large signpost had been hammered into the ground beside the path, with arrows pointing towards the two long dormitory huts, the wide canteen building, and the small unit housing the toilets and showers.

And every single cabin appeared to have been damaged. Savagely. Deep ragged rips had been torn into the woodwork, slicing through wall and roof alike. It was amazing that any of them were still standing.

'Um. Storm damage,' said T-Rex.

'Storm damage? But this place looked like new last year. Are we actually allowed to be here?' asked Simon.

'Sure. Camp still good,' said T-Rex, but he didn't sound very convinced.

'These buildings are falling to *pieces!* Look at the hole in that one,' said Whippet enthusiastically, pointing to a particularly large split that ran along the roof of the boys' dormitory. Whippet was becoming increasingly excited, the shattered scenery firing his imagination.

'That nothing. Want see deep gouge? Try arm-wrestle woolly mammoth. Them tusks *sharp!*'

T-Rex let out a barking laugh and slapped Whippet on the shoulder, almost knocking him off his feet. Whippet's eyes glazed over. His wide-eyed expression was

replaced with a sleepy smile that spread
slowly across his face. Simon watched him.
Whippet looked at his shoulder, where
T-Rex had just touched him, muttered the
words, 'Mammoth . . . brilliant,' then
reached for his rucksack and pulled out his
sketchpad and pencil. His hand was moving

on auto-pilot, the thought of T-Rex arm-wrestling a woolly mammoth seemingly too much inspiration for his comic-drawing-obsessed brain to ignore. He began to scribble.

T-Rex watched him draw for a moment, one eyebrow raised, then he cast his gaze over the buildings.

'Okay, so camp need love. New challenge – woodwork! Group fix camp.' Even cavemen had standards.

He strode off towards the nearby tree line, with a final shout over his shoulder.

'T-Rex get wood for repairs. Kids choose beds. No fighting.'

The group split into girls and boys and headed for separate cabins. Simon knew he should probably join the others but he couldn't. Not yet. This was wrong. The damaged campsite was dangerous somehow.

He didn't know why, but he could feel it, and it scared him.

The rain fell a little harder. Another bang and crack, further off this time. Lightning and thunder. Thunder and lightning.

A strange sensation tingled up Simon's spine. It was something he hadn't felt since his run-in with the Snotticus. Once upon a time such a tingling shiver would simply have meant he was cold, but a lot had changed in the past fortnight. Now the shiver meant a story was coming.

Simon held his breath and waited to see what would happen.

Something snagged his foot. He bent down to find a kind of black ribbon caught around his trainer. It was shiny to touch, and slick with rain. Simon recognised it as a roll of photographic film – his mum had an old camera that still used film like that.

He held the strip up and squinted at it, but there wasn't enough light filtering through the clouds to see what pictures had been snapped.

Stuffing the roll of film into his pocket, he peered around the clearing. There were the other kids, heading inside the huts. There was Whippet, sitting on his backpack, ignoring the spitting rain as he drew frantically in his sketchbook. There was T-Rex, tearing a dead tree out of the ground with his bare hands.

And there was Joe Bloggs – the Limousine Kid – standing alone.

Staring up at the sky.

Simon heard a faint ripping sound, and all of a sudden the air seemed to push itself around him, like water rising and spilling from a bucket into which a large rock has been dropped. It felt strange, but then the

weather was acting pretty odd. *Must be a big storm coming*, thought Simon.

'T-Rex is an inspirational genius,' said Whippet, thrusting his picture underneath Simon's nose. Simon took the sketchbook as his friend continued. 'Did you know **FREAKY** is running a readers' art competition? I'm thinking this picture might be worth entering. But tell me, Mossy . . . is it *WEIRD* enough?'

Simon looked down at his friend's drawing of their fearless camp leader locked in a deadly clinch with a six-tonne hairy elephant. The beast looked a little bit like a

woolly mammoth, but it had been drawn in Whippet's unique style, which meant it now had six legs, a bandana tied around its head and words shaved into its fur that read 'Extinction Stinks'.

Simon studied the picture, then looked up at where Joe Bloggs had been standing. The boy had disappeared. He'd simply vanished.

The weather grew worse.

'Yes, Whippet,' said Simon. 'Weird is the right word. Let's go get unpacked.'

Simon and Whippet were surprised and delighted to discover that the inside of their dormitory was in a much better condition than the exterior. Two rows of neat bunk beds sat on either side of the room. Apart from the unlucky kid who was going to have to sleep on the wet mattress directly beneath the gaping hole in the roof, each bed looked new and comfortable.

The boys unpacked their waterproof gear, grateful that they'd been told to bring jackets and wellington boots. If they were going to rebuild the camp in the pouring rain, then they'd need this stuff. As they unrolled their sleeping bags, the problem of the soggy bed came to a head. Understandably, no one wanted to volunteer, and soon tempers began to rise.

'Look, I'm the oldest here, so I get to say who sleeps where,' said Will Barnstable (**FREAKY** Fiend), and he puffed out his chest like a penguin as if to prove his point. (Simon knew that was not how penguins proved a point, though. They just hit each other with fish.)

'You're only older than me by ten days,' said Nate Rumble (bus bully and **FEARLESS** Fanatic). 'I should decide who gets the loser's bunk because I'm the fastest runner.'

There was a lot of nodding and murmured agreement from the rest of the group. Even Simon had to concede that being a fast runner was more impressive than being old.

'*Nyah, nyah, I can run fast. Nyah, nyah, nyah, I've got feet*,' mumbled Whippet.

Nate turned to stare across the

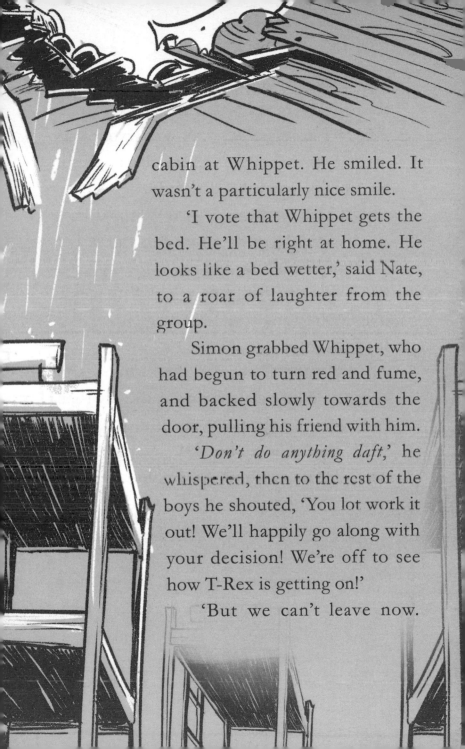

cabin at Whippet. He smiled. It wasn't a particularly nice smile.

'I vote that Whippet gets the bed. He'll be right at home. He looks like a bed wetter,' said Nate, to a roar of laughter from the group.

Simon grabbed Whippet, who had begun to turn red and fume, and backed slowly towards the door, pulling his friend with him.

'*Don't do anything daft,*' he whispered, then to the rest of the boys he shouted, 'You lot work it out! We'll happily go along with your decision! We're off to see how T-Rex is getting on!'

'But we can't leave now.

They're all inside – they'll definitely give me the bed! You heard Nate,' moaned Whippet.

'Not necessarily . . . Not everyone was in there,' said Simon, as they walked outside. He stopped and looked around.

'What's up, Mossy?' said Whippet.

'If you're talking about this camp, I'm not sure. Something strange happened here, and it happened recently. But let's tackle one mystery at a time – namely, where did Joe Bloggs go?'

Another flash of lightning. And another. Whippet frowned at the sky then cast a glance back at the dormitory.

'I don't know,' he said, scratching his head. 'He was with us when T-Rex went off to gather wood . . .'

'And now he's vanished. I think we should keep an eye on that boy,' said Simon.

At that precise moment T-Rex returned to the camp carrying a tree trunk on each shoulder. All thoughts of Joe Bloggs and wet beds were washed aside as the group got down to the serious business of woodwork. For most of them it was the first time they'd been put in charge of a saw, a hammer, a ladder or even a tape measure. Excitement bubbled around the camp, laughter mixing with the sound of construction (and the occasional scream) as the kids set about patching up the damaged buildings in their own unique way. What would have been a boring task if set by a teacher or parent, became infinitely more exciting when shared with friends and overseen by a caveman. T-Rex was less interested in woodworking in a professional way, and more interested in encouraging the children to make their own improvements.

The hours rolled past and by late afternoon the camp was no longer creepy. It was

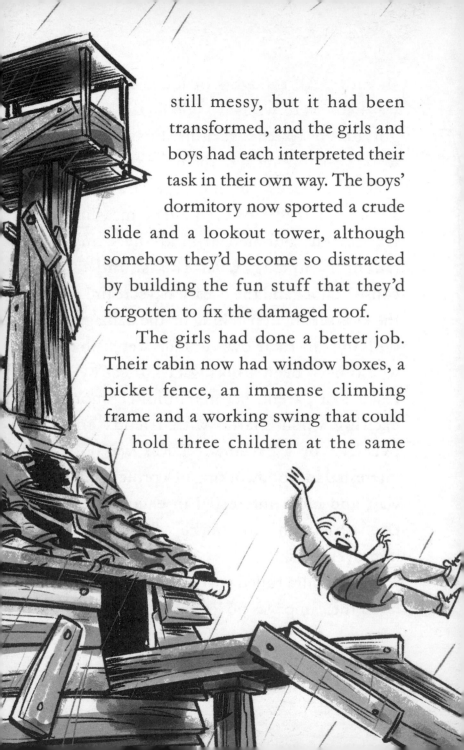

still messy, but it had been transformed, and the girls and boys had each interpreted their task in their own way. The boys' dormitory now sported a crude slide and a lookout tower, although somehow they'd become so distracted by building the fun stuff that they'd forgotten to fix the damaged roof.

The girls had done a better job. Their cabin now had window boxes, a picket fence, an immense climbing frame and a working swing that could hold three children at the same

time. They'd even found a tow rope in the camp bus to complete the swing.

T-Rex beamed with pleasure as he surveyed their finished efforts.

'Camp done. Camp great! T-Rex proud.' And with a big grin to the group he announced that the rest of the day was free time, and that dinner would be served at seven around the campfire. There wasn't actually a lot of the day left but that wasn't going to stop anyone from having fun.

'Kids explore, but stay out of wood.'

As the others drifted away to set up goals for a game of football, Simon massaged his sore hands. He hadn't done so much manual work since he'd last helped his dad improve their treehouse.

'You want to join in?' he asked Whippet, nodding towards the football pitch.

'No, Mossy. Everyone's busy. I think now would be the *perfect* moment for you and I to practise a little thing I like to call . . . your SUPERPOWER!'

Simon swallowed, smiled feebly, then followed his friend.

How was he going to explain to Whippet that his superpower was . . . um . . . super *broken?*

CHAPTER 6

EVOLUTION OF A HERO

When they were absolutely certain that no one was watching, Simon and Whippet snuck behind the girls' dormitory. It was the furthest cabin from the clearing in which the football game was already dissolving into a combination of rugby, football and free-for-all wrestling. As far as Simon could tell the girls were winning, but that was unsurprising. Girls had a tendency to play dirty when you least expected it. Just ask Lucy, Simon thought.

As they watched, Danica picked up the ball, leapt over the fallen figure of Ben Chub (**FEARLESS** Fanatic) and sprinted away from the pack, leaving even speedy Nate in her wake.

'Wow . . . that girl is pretty fast,' said Simon.

'Pretty mean too,' said Whippet, but before Simon could ask him what he meant, Whippet coughed. 'Enough distractions! Let's focus and power up!'

Simon sat on a tree stump as Whippet pulled a piece of chalk from his pocket and began to sketch hastily on the back wall of the hut.

'Okay, bear with me. *This* is T-Rex, right? He represents prehistoric civilisation,' said Whippet as he drew a crude chalk picture of their muscular camp leader on the wood. 'And *this* is your average modern human being.'

Another picture took shape. It was a pizza delivery boy with a dozy expression who appeared to be picking his nose with a long finger. Whippet continued to scribble.

'And *this*, Mossy . . . this is you.'

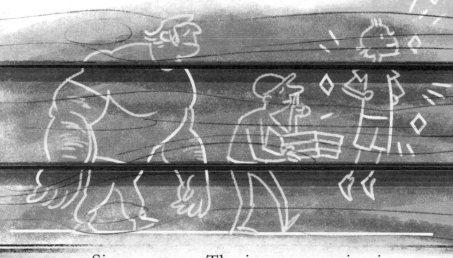

Simon sat up. The image emerging in the chalk looked a bit like Simon, but also nothing like Simon whatsoever. True, he was wearing Simon's shorts and T-shirt, but he also seemed to be floating two feet above the ground and was surrounded by beams of light and stars and swirling mist and stuff.

'What we've got here,' said Whippet, gesturing at the line-up, 'is called *evolution*, my friend, and you are the next link in the chain! A real-life, genuine superhero. Which is the coolest thing that has ever happened to the world, and more importantly, to us! Now, show me what you've got.'

Simon swallowed.

'What? Er, you mean . . . right now?'

'Right here, right now. Try to freeze me in place with the power of your words! *Stop time!*' said Whippet with a grin.

'I don't think it works like that . . . It's n-n-not that easy,' stuttered Simon, averting his gaze from his friend.

'Come on, give it a go! Tell me one of your tall, tall tales!'

Whippet dropped to the grass cross-legged, and gazed at Simon with a mixture of anticipation and excitement. Simon's embarrassment immediately began to bubble up like soup on a hot stove. He had never been more certain of anything in his life than that Whippet's experiment was about to end in failure. But his friend wasn't going to take no for an answer, and who knew? Perhaps this time – roughly the four hundredth time trying since their sewer battle – perhaps *this* time it would work.

Perhaps.

Simon emptied his mind, which wasn't all that hard. Then he tried to search for a single loose thread, something that could spark his imagination. He needed a hook, but after a few moments there was still nothing to snag his interest.

In desperation he looked around and his eyes settled on Whippet's scribbles on the cabin wall. Simon marvelled at the perfect comic representation of T-Rex and the drippy pizza boy. What that boy could do with a single piece of chalk was remarkable, he thought.

No, more than remarkable. It was almost magic.

Ding.

. . . Once upon a time there lived a little boy. He was normal in every way except that he had never spoken a word in his life. The doctors didn't know if he was unable to speak or if he simply chose NOT to speak, but whatever the reason, he had never uttered a single thing to anyone about anything.

For the boy did not need words to communicate

with the world . . . he only needed his magic chalk . . .

Whippet leaned forwards. Simon's heart swelled with hope. Was he being pulled in? Had he been hypnotised by the story? Was this the way it —

'Magic chalk! Ha, that's excellent! Okay, Mossy, so what could it do? Teleport him away from trouble? Make him invisible? Vanquish his enemies with laser beams?'

Simon paused, his mouth opened but no words came out. Whippet's ideas had derailed his thinking and the beginning of the story that he'd sensed was now retreating to the very back of this mind.

And just like that, it was gone.

Whippet frowned as his friend slumped down beside him.

'Why have you stopped? That was just getting good,' said Whippet.

Simon took a deep breath.

'No it wasn't. It wasn't going anywhere. I'm sorry, pal, but I can't do it. I just can't repeat the trick.'

'What? You're kidding!' said Whippet. Then, because it felt like a major moment that required a rather more serious response, he added: 'Bums.'

'Yup,' said Simon dejectedly. He hugged his knees. There really wasn't much more to say.

The pair sat in silence for a while. Simon studied the ground while Whippet absentmindedly rolled the piece of chalk around in his fingers. He stared at it for a long time before speaking.

'You know what I'd do if *I* had a magic piece of chalk? I'd get my revenge on all the Nate Rumbles of the world,' he said. There was an edge to his voice that Simon hadn't heard before. His friend could be moody, and he was genuinely a bit odd, but he'd never been mean. He'd never been cruel.

'You *do* have magic chalk. And pencils and pens. Look at your drawings. They're incredible! Some of them are so lifelike they could be real,' said Simon, gesturing to the wall of the cabin.

'Being able to draw well is *not* a super skill,' said Whippet. 'I'm talking about laser beams, invisibility, REAL power! With all that good stuff I could make every bully suffer. Strike a blow for the underdogs.' Whippet jumped to his feet and swung his chalk around like a sword.

'No you wouldn't, Whippet. You read **FREAKY** and **FEARLESS** every week – you know what happens to power-mad loonies. Their plans backfire and they end up in prison, or worse, a pile of smoking ashes. Every time! Superpowers aren't supposed to be used for revenge.'

Whippet folded his arms and scowled at his friend.

'Yeah, well, what would *I* know about that, Mossy?'

Now *this* was an awkward moment.

Was Whippet jealous of his storytelling skill? thought Simon. Quite frankly, he was welcome to it. Simon didn't know if it would ever work again, but either way, he felt certain it was largely useless.

'What are you two doing back here?'

Whippet and Simon spun round so fast that they collided with each other. Standing beside the corner of the cabin two figures could be seen. Danica and Joe.

'Are you hiding . . . from me?' Danica asked, looking directly at Whippet.

'Er, hiding –' began Whippet nervously.

'Yes, and you found us! Congratulations,' said Simon hurriedly, interrupting his friend. 'So that makes you the winners.'

Danica raised an eyebrow at Simon then turned back to face Whippet. 'Well, anyway, we've been sent to round everyone up. Come on.'

Joe's face was still hidden by his hat but Simon was sure he could see a grin on the new boy's face. He was staring at Whippet's sketch of the evolution of a hero. Before

Simon could say anything, the roaring voice of T-Rex tore through the quiet of the camp with a mighty *'FIRE GOOD, DINNER READY! GROUND WET, SO WEAR WELLIES!'*

As the four rounded the cabin, Whippet nudged Simon.

'You *still* think we're safe?' he said, pointing to Danica and Joe. 'The forces of evil. Like I keep telling you. They can find us anywhere!'

Simon laughed and shook his head as he trudged towards the glow of the campfire.

CHAPTER 7

SAUSAGES AND SCARES

You could say one thing for T-Rex: the caveman knew how to build a campfire. Despite the fact that the clouds continued to shower the camp with a steady downpour, and the lightning flashed constantly over the distant wood, the rest of the group already sitting at the bonfire felt nothing but warmth and comfort.

The towering inferno T-Rex had constructed was so immense that the rain simply evaporated before it fell on their heads! The other children were already sitting on large fallen logs arranged like benches around the fireside. As far as the kids were concerned, being out in the rain here was far better than cosying up at home with the central heating. After all, you couldn't cook marshmallows on a radiator.

As Simon, Whippet, Joe and Danica approached the group the scent hit them like a slap.

'Hmmmm . . . Mossy . . . can you smell that? That's . . . that's incredible,' said Whippet, sniffing at the air frantically and licking his lips.

Simon's nose had also been filled with the rich, wonderful aroma of frying sausages, burgers, chicken wings and

buttered corn on the cob. The boys grabbed paper plates and hurried to queue up beside the sizzling barbecue before everything disappeared.

Joe Bloggs was already waiting in front of them.

'Look who's rejoined the group,' whispered Simon to Whippet. As they watched, Joe loaded his plate then moved away to sit on the far side of the fire. He peacefully dipped a sausage into a big dollop of ketchup and chewed quietly, his head barely moving beneath his cap. He clearly had no desire to join the others.

Simon shook his head and returned to the log benches with his own plate. He sat down beside Whippet, who was pretending not to listen to Danica. The girl was trying to explain to Whippet that, in her opinion, conspiracy theories were largely made up,

and that Whippet would be better off ignoring the fantasies and focusing on what was real and right in front of him.

Good luck with that, thought Simon. Across the circle a different animated discussion was underway. The subject was a favourite among the children of Lake Shore: who would win in a wrestling match – T-Rex or Captain Armstrong. After a lot of arguing they settled on a draw, but all agreed that a battle between a caveman and a pirate would be extremely cool to watch.

Night gradually closed around the fire like a hug. When dinner had been consumed and all the plates returned to the canteen – and certain boys and girls had stopped groaning from having tried to eat their own body weight in sausages – T-Rex rose from his seat and spread his arms wide. Lit by the fire, with embers floating around him and the stars twinkling above, he looked more like a caveman than ever.

'It time . . . time for GHOST STORIES!' boomed T-Rex.

The clearing fell silent but you could HEAR the grins spreading. *This* was why so many of the kids loved the Explorers' Camp. It was the chance to scare, and be scared, by a spooky tale. And the **FREAKY** comic fans were the keenest of all.

'*Brilliant*,' said Whippet.

'Oh, yeah, and T-Rex's are particularly horrible,' said Simon in nervous anticipation.

'Who go first?' asked T-Rex, looking around the gathering. No one raised their hands.

Then Whippet's arm lifted into the air. Whippet stared up at his hand as if he'd never seen it before. Then he realised it had been hoisted by Danica.

'I'd like to hear Whippet tell a story,' she said with a smile. 'He has a unique imagination.'

From the other side of the campfire Nate let out a chortle.

'Sure, Danica. But only if by "unique" you actually mean MENTAL!'

Whippet flushed. Then he shook his head frantically and pulled his arm free.

'No way! Er, no thanks! I draw the pictures, I don't tell the stories,' he said in a

panic. 'That's Mossy's thing. Get *him* to tell a story.'

Simon shot his friend a look. An hour earlier he'd confessed to being unable to use his storytelling power and here was his best friend dropping him right in the deep end! Whippet shrugged apologetically, but that wasn't much help to Simon.

Thankfully T-Rex stepped in to solve everyone's problems.

'T-Rex start. T-Rex got scary story to end all scary stories.'

Nate suddenly jumped to his feet.

'Mr Recks, I have to use the toilet,' he said, dancing from foot to foot. Whippet sniggered.

'Take torch. Camp dark. Nate not have accident,' said T-Rex, then threw a *huge* flashlight to Nate. It was T-Rex-sized and the weight of it almost knocked Nate off his feet. He switched it on and a beam as wide and as bright as a lighthouse shot out, blinding everyone who looked at it. Nate seemed to take particular pleasure picking out Whippet.

'Oops! Sorry, Whippet. Haha! Back soon,' said Nate, then scurried away.

'Grrr . . . that kid is driving me nuts,' said Whippet, blinking to try to clear his eyes.

Simon gripped his friend's shoulder supportively.

'Try to ignore him,' said Simon. 'He can't help being an idiot.'

T-Rex had stood up and was circling the group, flickering in and out of view in the firelight like an immense spectre.

'Nate sad to miss this one. This terrifying tale of

WAILING WOOD LUNATIC!'

Simon leaned forwards.

'On dark night like tonight, twenty-three kids arrive at lonely camp. They looking forward to fun and adventure. Happy to be away from home. Happy to be living wild. But kids NOT happy when they hear news on radio: *dangerous lunatic escaped from nearby prison . . .'*

T-Rex paused. Twenty-two mouths hung open. Whippet was drooling, his bad mood ebbing away as the story unfolded.

'. . . a prison for *insane* criminals with thirst for *BLOOD!*'

Everyone whooped in delight. There was a flash of light in the sky. Then a crack of thunder. *Even the weather is getting excited*, thought Simon. He'd never seen so many bolts of lightning in his life.

T-Rex continued, stalking around the fire, the light throwing his shadow this way and that.

'Horror start on first night. Children sit by fire . . . facing flames . . . listen to story. No one pay attention to forest, then scarred face appear from shadows . . . but no one notice.'

T-Rex began to slowly circle the fire the other way, his hand shadow moving, the jaw opening and closing.

FLASH! FLASH! Followed by a double crack of thunder.

Simon looked up, but the light from the fire was so intense it masked everything, even the stars.

T-Rex continued his tale.

'Figure with scarred face creep towards camp . . . hide in shadows . . . no one notice. Slide up behind smallest boy . . . *still* no one notice!'

A hand gripped Whippet's knee. He let out a yelp of surprise before he realised it was just Danica.

'Sorry,' she said nervously, with an apologetic smile.

Whippet gulped and tried to act totally cool as T-Rex continued. The caveman walked slowly across the fireside clearing towards Joe Bloggs, the boy appearing largely unimpressed by his spooky tale. *He doesn't look even slightly scared*, thought Simon. In fact, he was the only child not desperately peering over their shoulder to check the surroundings for escaped, insane criminals.

'No one see . . . no one care. Then, with sound like flint sharpened on stone, voice whisper from the scarred face . . .'

Every child held their breath. Even the rain appeared to pause momentarily in midair.

T-Rex grinned and threw his head back.

'. . . and voice say –'

SCREEEEEEEEEEEEEE-BOOOOM!

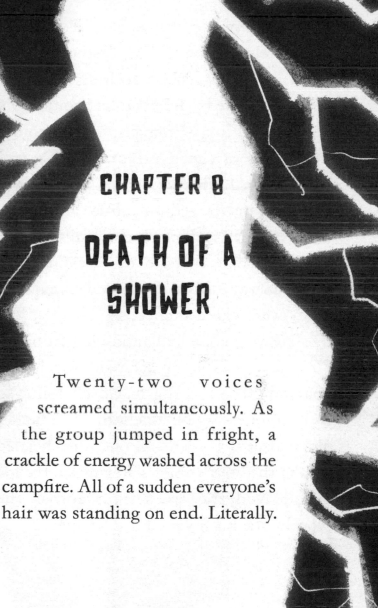

CHAPTER 8

DEATH OF A SHOWER

Twenty-two voices screamed simultaneously. As the group jumped in fright, a crackle of energy washed across the campfire. All of a sudden everyone's hair was standing on end. Literally.

It would have been laughable if it wasn't so completely terrifying. For, despite Simon's initial suspicion, the screeching noise had not been made by T-Rex. It had come from behind the group. From one of the cabins.

'What in the name of **FREAKY** was *THAT?*' said Whippet, trying and failing to pat down his frizzed-up hairdo.

'No idea,' said Simon truthfully, feeling his own crazy tufts. 'I don't even know where it came from. It seemed to explode from everywhere at once.'

T-Rex grabbed a flaming log from the fire to use as a replacement torch and charged off to investigate, closely followed by everyone else. No one wanted to be left alone after that scare. As one, they headed first to the boys' cabin. T-Rex raised the log and played the fire's light across the woodwork but everything seemed to be normal. Next they moved to the girls' dormitory. Then the canteen. The results were the same. Nothing was out of place. Not a single sign of disturbance.

'What about the shower hut?' said Simon. 'We haven't checked that.'

T-Rex nodded and they moved back across the campsite.

'Er, Mr Reeks?' said a ginger-haired boy called Jason Tyke. 'Where *is* the shower hut?'

'Shower over –' began T-Rex, then promptly stopped talking as his flaming torch passed over the area where the shower and toilet block had previously been situated.

There was very little left to see.

In place of the building was a deep smoking crater. Burst water pipes rose from the charred ground, their contents erupting into the air like a fountain. A single battered toilet sat in the middle of the hole. Propped on top of it — his shorts around his ankles, his face as white as a sheet, and his hair standing upright — sat Nate Rumble, clutching the shattered remains of T-Rex's massive flashlight.

A tall, rather serious-looking girl called Emma Skettle stared at Nate in horror.

Then she turned to T-Rex with a worried expression.

'Mr Recks . . . is . . . is *that* what happens if you eat too many sausages?'

The rest of the group giggled nervously, although Simon could tell from their faces that at least half of them were wondering the same thing. The sound of their laughter seemed to bring Nate back to his senses. He pulled his shorts up and T-Rex helped him to scramble out of the crater.

'What happen?' asked the camp leader kindly, kneeling beside the shivering boy.

'I-I-I don't know,' stuttered Nate. 'I f-f-finished my b-b-business but as I was about to flush there was a screaming, w-w-wailing sound . . . and the n-n-next thing I know I'm s-s-sitting in a smoking hole in the g-g-*ground!*'

'Hmmm, sounds like blocked pipe,' said T-Rex.

'That's some blockage, sir,' said Whippet, looking around at the destruction.

'You right. T-Rex blame fast food. Not enough fibre. Me have similar problem with brontosaurus diet.'

The giant camp leader patted Nate kindly on the shoulder.

'Ghost stories wait. Me shut off water, kids go to bed. Early start tomorrow an' remember – dirty wellies stay outside cabin. We fix camp, so you no make new mess.'

Nate was led away by the others, all of whom showed an extreme keenness to discover exactly what it was like to be at the centre of an explosion. Then someone tapped Simon lightly on his shoulder.

'Psst . . . *Mossy*,' said Whippet. 'What's *he* up to?'

Little Joe Bloggs had climbed down into the hole and was kneeling and rooting through the smouldering remains of the

shower block. As Whippet and Simon watched, Joe stood and raised something into the air. Gripped in his hand was a feather . . . a single bone-white feather. Joe shoved it into his jacket pocket and marched away, back in the direction of the boys' cabin.

'Collecting feathers in the middle of all this? Are you going to tell me that's not freaky behaviour?' asked Whippet.

'It *is* weird. And that's the first evidence I've seen that there even *are* any birds here,' said Simon.

He frowned. Cocked his head to one side. And then he heard it. A snort. A shuffle. A rustle from the treeline. Simon froze.

'Whippet. We're . . . we're not alone.'

Whippet clapped his hands and danced a little crazy jig on the spot.

'Finally you believe me! All these years I've been saying it. The government doesn't want anyone to know but we are NOT alone,' he said joyfully.

Simon held a hand over his friend's mouth.

'Keep it down. I'm not talking about *aliens*,' he whispered, 'but there's something hiding in those bushes.'

Simon nodded towards the wood. This time they both heard the rustling. Simon gave Whippet his best *back-me-up-on-this-one-buddy* look and removed his hand from his mouth. Whippet didn't look particularly happy but he nodded, and the boys tiptoed towards the forest. Reaching the bushes at the edge of the campsite they paused. The rustling was so loud they were surprised the whole camp hadn't run over to investigate, but by then everyone was in their cabins.

'Ready?' mouthed Simon.

'No,' mouthed Whippet.

'Good. Go,' mouthed Simon, and in unison the boys dived through the undergrowth.

They rolled and came up together, side by side. If the situation had been a little less nerve-wracking, Simon would have cheered, for it was a pretty cool move. But as things transpired, neither boy made a sound. They simply stopped moving. Stopped breathing. Stopped understanding.

Standing before them, as real as the towering trees and the weeds that snagged at their wellies, was a woolly mammoth.

Not just any woolly mammoth but a woolly mammoth with six legs, a bandana tied around its head, and words shaved into its fur that read '*Extinction Stinks*'.

CHAPTER 9

THE REAL JOE BLOGGS

'Whippet?' whispered Simon.

'Murgle,' mumbled Whippet.

'Buddy! Little *help* here,' whispered Simon.

'Wurgly murgle,' mumbled Whippet, his mouth moving like he was talking through a sock.

'*SNAP OUT OF IT,*' hissed Simon.

'Wurlgy ... ah, I mean, woolly! It's a woolly mammoth, Mossy! *It's MY woolly mammoth*,' said Whippet, coming to his senses.

The clearing was still. No one moved a muscle. Not the boys, not the mammoth. In fact, the animal looked extremely peaceful. It wasn't in the slightest bit bothered by their presence, and as if to prove the point it stretched up its trunk to rip a mouthful of leaves from the lowest branches of the surrounding trees.

'How is this possible?' said Simon, looking at his best friend in confusion.

Whippet's head was shaking from side to side like a car's dashboard toy. He looked more annoyed than scared.

'Mammoths are all dead. They're long gone, and even if one had survived, frozen in a block of ice or something, well . . . it

wouldn't have six legs, would it?' said Whippet.

Simon gripped his friend's arm. He needed to distract him before he went into shock.

'The legs are weird, I agree, but how about the bandana? Or the words in its fur?' he asked.

Simon took a deep breath. His power to stop monsters in their tracks appeared to be temporarily out of action. The boys just weren't prepared for confronting a mammoth. Simon began to edge slowly back through the bushes and onto open ground. Whippet followed him, emerging a moment later, his eyes still locked in the direction of the mammoth. 'How do those legs coordinate when it runs?' he said.

'That is certainly a question worth thinking about, and we are definitely in need of some answers,' said Simon and they began to jog back towards the campsite. Simon reached their cabin first, only to discover he was all on his own. Turning round, he spotted Whippet standing beside the crater. He appeared to be shaking.

'Whippet? What's wrong?' said Simon, walking up to his friend.

'I . . . I did this,' said Whippet, staring mournfully at the destruction.

'What are talking about? You don't know that.'

'*I* did this,' said Whippet through gritted teeth. 'Somehow, I drew that thing and brought it to life and it attacked Nate. I said I wanted to hurt the bullies, remember, I wanted to teach them a lesson . . . and . . . and I did!'

Simon shook his head. Even if he ignored the impossible, and Whippet HAD brought the creature to life, the facts didn't add up. The mammoth they had just met didn't seem like the sort of creature that could destroy an entire building. Not on its own, anyway. And then there was the small matter of the bone-white feather found at the scene of the crime. Where had that come from? If it wasn't the mammoth that had attacked Nate, then that meant there was something *else* lurking in the shadows . . .

'We don't know what happened. We need to talk to an expert,' said Simon.

'Why would T-Rex believe us?' said Whippet miserably. 'It sounds like a stupid joke. *What do you do if a mammoth sits on your toilet? . . . Build another toilet . . .*'

Simon paused. He contemplated talking to their camp leader. Unlike Whippet, he felt pretty certain that T-Rex probably *would* believe them, but he also knew the caveman

couldn't help. Captain Armstrong had confirmed as much in the basement of the Shipshape Shop. T-Rex and the Captain had their secrets and their reasons for not helping, but they didn't seem ready to share them, so the boys were on their own . . . or were they?

'You know, T-Rex is not the expert I had in mind. I think we should have a quiet chat with Joe Bloggs,' said Simon.

'Joe?' said Whippet as they struck out for the boys' dormitory. 'It's going to be difficult to talk to Joe about anything, what with him having lost his voice, remember? Of course, we might be able to find his voice inside that giant holdall he was dragging. That thing's big enough to hold just about anything!'

And there it was: the answer. So obvious once you knew what you were looking for. Simon had been looking at the right problem in the wrong way.

'It would be hard to talk to Joe,' said Simon, 'if his story was *true*. Come on, Whippet!'

They reached the cabin, struggled out of their muddy wellingtons and dumped them with the mountain of other wet boots on the cabin porch. Inside, a heated Devil Jets card game was underway between Will and Jason and the room was filled with the noise of celebrations and insults. Joe was nowhere to be seen.

Simon scanned the beds. Sitting on the top bunk, beneath the hole in the roof they had forgotten to repair, someone had cunningly erected a tent.

'Wow — smart kid,' said Whippet. 'I can't believe any of this lot would think to pack a tent when they knew we were going to be sleeping indoors.'

'They didn't,' whispered Simon, as the pair climbed up to the top bunk and threw open the front tent flaps, 'but *SHE* did!'

Whippet gasped. Simon grinned. Then stopped. Both boys raised their hands as a handheld pocket crossbow emerged from the darkness of the tent, pointed directly at them. A small hand poked out of the gloom alongside the weapon and a curled finger beckoned them inside. The boys obediently crawled into the tent.

'*LUCY?*' exclaimed Whippet in disbelief. 'But, but, but . . .'

'Stop dribbling and keep your voice down, moron,' whispered Lucy Shufflebottom in her usual friendly manner.

'But, but, but . . .' continued Whippet.

'Simon, I'm warning you – I *will* hurt him.'

Simon zipped the tent flaps closed. This was *not* a meeting the other scouts needed to know about.

Joe Bloggs, it turned out, was *not* Joe Bloggs. Joe Bloggs was in fact Lucy Shufflebottom, smallest explorer on Earth, saviour of Simon's little sister Ruby, fearless monster hunter and the most dangerous red-haired nine-year-old girl to ever wield a loaded weapon! She was also, apparently, a master of disguise.

Lucy tossed her crossbow onto the pillow and sat down. She gave Simon a long, mean stare.

'Okay, what gave me away?' said Lucy in annoyance.

'Well,' said Simon, 'you were acting pretty weird when we first arrived. And then, while everyone else was heading to bed, you stopped to grab a large white feather from the crater, which was odd. *Then* Whippet helped me realise that not being able to speak meant we wouldn't know you were a girl, and the same goes for the cap that covers your entire face, which was a clever disguise. But your holdall was the final giveaway. I've only ever met one person with a bag that big.'

The holdall in question was lying open on the bed. Inside the boys could clearly see Lucy's famous rucksack.

'Very clever,' said Lucy.

'Thanks,' said Simon with a grin.

Lucy gave a long sigh. Whippet looked from one to the other.

'What are you DOING here, Lucy?' he said. 'You realise this is the *boys'* cabin? And why are you wearing that disguise?'

'I'm not here because of stupid boys,' said Lucy in a fierce whisper. 'Well, I am, but only YOU TWO. I needed to keep an eye on you both *without* getting into a whole "reunion" thing – which is why I was in disguise! I'm not exactly big on hugs.'

Lucy set about rummaging through her giant rucksack, then pulled out her prize. Whippet flinched, remembering the bazooka she had brought on their last adventure. Thankfully this item was a lot smaller – in fact it was just a rolled-up comic.

'Did you chumps read Issue 2287 of **FEARLESS**?' said Lucy, throwing the comic on the bed in front of the boys.

Simon looked down at the comic. Ah. That issue. The one with the cover of the barbarian red-haired warrior. Simon frowned. The character looked familiar, somehow. He looked at the cover again. Then he looked at Lucy. Then the cover. Seeing them side by side, the similarity was unmistakable.

'Stop staring at me like that and turn to page twenty-two. See anyone you recognise?' said Lucy.

Both boys knew what was coming but they flipped to the right page anyway.

There, portrayed in stunning comic detail, was the concluding instalment of the *Batty Beasts* story. The one that ended with a picture of the *Snotticus Galavantia* . . . the monster they had fought in the sewer.

Simon and Whippet exchanged a look. Simon picked up the comic.

'Yeah, we saw it. We thought maybe the artist had used a photograph of the Snotticus as a reference or something. Or that maybe it wasn't actually a monster, like you said, but just some really rare animal. We even tried looking for another picture of it. We searched online and in some wildlife books.'

'No luck, huh? Of *course* it was a monster! And here we are again.

A spooky wood. An exploding toilet. A freaky lightning storm that won't end . . .' said Lucy.

'. . . *a woolly mammoth*,' added Whippet.

Lucy shot him a look. It was almost as sharp as the bolt loaded into her crossbow.

'Don't be daft, Whippet.'

'I'm not,' said Whippet. 'There's a living, breathing mammoth out there in the woods – I should know, I drew it!'

'We don't have time for your fantasies!' snapped Lucy.

Simon shook his head.

'He's telling the truth, Lucy. I saw it too. I've seen enough pictures to know a woolly mammoth when it looks me in the eye.'

Lucy glared from one boy to the next, then back again. Simon wilted under the intensity of her look.

'I can't tell whether you two are being

stupid or serious, but just listen,' said Lucy. 'You boys are on an accidental collision course with something big. Yesterday I intercepted a message on my police radio scanner. It was a potential lead on another monstrous target. Some lady called Madeline Fortune complaining about a giant rampaging bird. Can you guess where the message came from?' said Lucy.

'You have a police radio scanner?' said Whippet, ignoring the question.

'Of course I do. Anyway, the message came from right here, in Wailing Wood. Some sort of huge bird has been terrorising the local birdwatchers and scaring off the wildlife.'

Lucy dug the giant feather out of her backpack.

'From now on I'm not leaving your side. Not until I get to the bottom of this new mystery!'

CHAPTER 10

THE FOOTWEAR THIEF

As Simon and Whippet tried once again to convince Lucy of the very real presence of a mammoth in the undergrowth their secret meeting was cut short. T-Rex arrived to announce that if the boys didn't stop making enough noise to wake the dead, let alone the girls in their cabin, he would confiscate everyone's games, comics and sweets. He also promised to feed them a breakfast of woodlice, poison ivy and horse dung. Serious stuff, and despite the fact that no one had seen any horses in the woods, the thought of woodlice and poison ivy on toast was enough to send Simon, Whippet, 'Joe' and the other boys scurrying back to their bunks.

But Simon couldn't get to sleep. His mind was filled with an ever-increasing list of questions. Had Whippet really brought one of his drawings to life? Where had his own power gone? How did the creators of the **FEARLESS** comic know about the Snotticus? What was this 'giant rampaging bird' Lucy was chasing and where were all these monsters coming from? And what about Whippet's mammoth – would it be okay out there, all alone in the dark? It had seemed like quite a friendly animal and he didn't want it to come to any harm.

The answers did not appear with the arrival of morning. Nor did they materialise as Simon washed his face beneath a grey sky, using a broken water pipe that T-Rex had pulled from the ground and rebuilt as an outdoor tap. The answers didn't come as Simon got dressed, or when he sat down for breakfast in the canteen.

Whippet chewed absentmindedly on his scrambled eggs. He was equally clueless.

'Sorry, Mossy, I've got nothing,' he said, through a large mouthful. 'All I know is giant bird or no giant bird, if Lucy's *here* then we're in trouble. She has a police radio scanner. She attracts danger!'

'Yeah . . . but so do we,' said Simon, nodding towards the window, through which the crater of the shower hut could be seen.

'Do you think I should apologise to Nate for what happened last night?' said Whippet.

Simon looked at Nate, who was sitting on a far table with his friends. He seemed a lot quieter than before, which was no bad thing in Simon's opinion. Nate's hair was still standing on end and as he silently pushed his eggs around his plate, his companions excitedly discussed the action of the previous evening. The general feeling was that T-Rex's scary story was a true one and that there had to be something shocking hiding in the undergrowth, just waiting to pounce on some poor unsuspecting kid.

You're not wrong, thought Simon, *but you probably weren't expecting a six-legged mammoth.*

He patted Whippet on the back.

'Your apology can wait until we know what really happened, buddy. Even I'm finding the thought of a living, breathing comic drawing hard to believe. And I saw it! Plus, there's that giant feather . . .'

Suddenly 'Joe Bloggs' and Danica appeared and proceeded to sit down on the opposite side of the table.

'Mind if we join you?' said Danica, making herself comfortable.

'Do we have a choice?' mumbled Whippet.

'Not really,' said Danica with a soft smile. She picked up Whippet's sketchbook, which he'd left on the table beside his plate. 'Mind if I take a peek?'

Danica was already flipping through the pages before Whippet could decide on his answer.

'Hmm . . . uh-huh . . . interesting . . .' she said.

'*Interesting?*' said Whippet nervously.

She spun the book around. She was holding it open at the sketch of Whippet's mammoth. The boys sat very still. *Does she know?* thought Simon. *How could she know?*

'This picture, there's something about it,' said Danica.

'Er, yes? W-what about it, exactly?' asked Whippet, his eyes flitting from Simon to Lucy to Danica.

'Yes. I think, perhaps, it could do with

some colour. You know, to break up all that black.'

Whippet blinked and looked at the picture. Simon exhaled in relief. Their secret was safe. For now. Danica continued to study the drawing for a moment then returned to her breakfast.

'*Red* for the bandana. Just a thought,' said Danica, then dipped a hunk of sausage into a big blob of ketchup and popped it in her mouth.

Simon watched as Whippet frowned, staring first at her plate, then his picture. Then he dipped his little finger in his own ketchup and traced it over the mammoth's bandana. His frown disappeared and his eyes lit up. He looked almost happy.

'Red . . .' he said thoughtfully.

'Morning,' boomed T-Rex, interrupting everyone's thoughts. The camp leader was standing in the entrance to the canteen. 'Kids finish breakfast, prepare for hike! Today we get wild . . . hunt rare birds! Child spot rarest bird wins prize.'

There was a cheer from the group. T-Rex's prizes were renowned. Simon remembered last summer, when T-Rex had awarded Jermaine Flannel a flint battle axe for successfully jumping over a wide stream. Jermaine's parents were none too pleased, but their son treasured his trophy.

'Weather get worse. Bring coats and boots. Meet in ten minutes.'

Simon, Whippet and the others set off to grab their waterproofs. Running inside their cabin, the boys kicked off their trainers then headed back to the porch to grab their wellies. Whippet was the first to get there.

'Um . . .' he said, spinning on the spot. 'Where are they?'

All that remained of the mountain of wellies from the previous night was a muddy smear on the porch planking. Will Barnstable pointed a finger at Jason Tyke.

'Is this one of your practical jokes, Tyke?'

Jason held up his hands in confusion.

'Hey, don't look at me! I want to win that prize as much as anyone, but my wellies aren't here either. I'm not a cheat!'

While the boys squabbled, Lucy shouldered her huge backpack, moved to one side and beckoned Simon and Whippet. She slowly pulled the curled white feather from her pocket and gave it a waggle.

'What?' said Simon. 'Are you saying your mysterious "giant bird" had something to do with this? Birds don't steal shoes, Lucy.'

'Do you have another suspect?' she whispered back.

Simon nodded.

'Whippet's mammoth.'

'Not that again,' said Lucy.

'Come on,' said Simon. 'If a Snotticus can exist, a creature unlike anything on earth, a creature that collects *noses*, then is it that much of stretch for a mammoth to steal shoes?'

Lucy chewed on her lip. Simon stuffed his hands in his pockets and waited for a reaction.

'I guess not,' she said, to both Simon and Whippet's surprise. Simon was about to push his argument further when his right hand closed around something. Something shiny.

He pulled out the roll of film. He'd completely forgotten about it. Holding it up to the overhead light of the cabin, he studied the images, one beside the other.

'Where did you find that?' said Lucy.

The photographs had been taken in a hurry. *Click click click.*

'It was right here in the . . . in the . . .' Simon's voice failed him.

'In the *what?*' said Whippet, leaning over his friend's shoulder. 'What is it? What can you see?'

Feathers. That was what Simon could see. A blur of white feathers. Swooping. Diving. Clearly a bird of some sort, but unrecognisable. Somebody had taken snap after snap after snap of the animal and not one of them was in focus. Simon could make out what appeared to be a pair of claws. Big claws belonging to a big bird.

He silently passed the film to Whippet and Lucy, who squabbled over who'd get to examine it first. Simon explained that he'd found the film in the camp clearing, when they'd first arrived. It seemed that Lucy's tip-off might be true. Perhaps there really was more than one monster waiting in the woods.

This camping trip was turning into one big muddy mystery, thought Simon. And now, thanks to their footwear thief, things were about to get *muddier!*

CHAPTER 11

THE WAY THROUGH WAILING WOOD

'Wet feet no problem. Hiking more fun when messy,' said T-Rex, as everyone gathered in the clearing wearing their trainers instead of their boots. 'Now we GO!'

With T-Rex out in front, the group set

off along an old footpath that wound away from the back of the campsite into Wailing Wood. Almost as soon as they crossed the treeline at the edge of the forest, weeds and moss sprang up to snare their trainers. Simon and Whippet looked around in concern. This was the exact spot where they'd found the mammoth, but the great woolly wonder was nowhere to be seen.

And soon it became difficult to see anything at all, as dark and twisted tree trunks closed in around them. Wailing Wood was living up to its reputation as a spooky spot. Despite the fact that it was ten o'clock in the morning, the lack of light in

the wood made it feel like midnight. Nervous conversations about spooks and escaped loonies began to spring up along the line of kids. Simon was more worried that at any moment Whippet's mammoth might decide to charge across their path. That would create a whole new level of terror!

What Wailing Wood was not living up to was its reputation as a home for winged animals.

'Er, Mr Recks, where are all the birds?' said Emma Skettle, when they stopped for a breather fifteen minutes later.

T-Rex didn't reply. Instead he simply cocked his head to one side and raised a giant fist to cup it round his ear. No one spoke. T-Rex lowered his hand. Something was bothering him.

'This strange,' he muttered. 'Wood silent.'

Another flash. Another bang. Simon jumped in surprise.

'Except lightning and thunder,' whispered Lucy, staring at Simon, who was trying hard to pretend that he had not just jumped in fright. She laughed.

'God, are boys always so *pathetic?*' she muttered as they marched on. While everyone else struggled to navigate the thick brambles, Lucy simply hacked her way through the undergrowth with her trusty machete.

'Not always,' said Simon.

'I'm sure we'd be much braver if we were each carrying a small arsenal of *weapons* on our back!' replied Whippet.

Simon rolled his eyes in anticipation of a squabble, but before the argument escalated to the point where Lucy introduced Whippet to the 'business end' of her machete, T-Rex stopped suddenly. Unprepared for the abrupt halt, Jason Tyke strode straight into the camp leader's back, then Danica stumbled into Jason, Nate blundered into Danica and so on, right down the line.

Whippet, Simon and Lucy managed to avoid the pile-up but did suffer from a chronic fit of giggles. Simon craned his neck to see what had happened.

'Only hero go further,' said T-Rex from the head of the queue. 'Path blocked by raging river! Rope bridge only way. Who dare go FIRST?'

Lucy, her cap pulled even further down over her face, barged her way through the others, pulling Simon and Whippet behind her.

'Volunteers – good! And new boy too,' said T-Rex, smiling as he moved to one side.

'Take care. Bridge old. Go *slow*.'

Simon and Whippet moved past, but T-Rex held a hand out to slow Lucy. He bent down to peer beneath the peak of her hat. He looked her in the eye.

'T-Rex serious. Be careful. Danger close. Me feel it.'

Simon turned at those words. They seemed innocent enough, but then Lucy gave T-Rex a knuckle-bump. That was *not* innocent. Did he know who she really was?

Whippet grabbed Simon's sleeve and pulled him back to the present. Their camp leader was not lying. Directly in their path lay a rickety bridge that looked about a million years old. Weak light played through the gap in the trees to

illuminate the grey river far below, which was indeed raging. Surging rapids bubbled as the water sped past. Whippet tentatively pressed a toe against the first moss-covered plank. It gave an ominous creak.

'Nope. Nuh-uh! *No way!* I am NOT going anywhere near that thiiiiiiiiiiiiiiiiing –'

His voice stretched into a high-pitched squeal as he found himself sliding uncontrollably across the mossy bridge. Lucy had decided to give him a helping hand (or two), slammed in the middle of his back.

'What is it with girls making decisions for me?' said Whippet, his voice quavering, as his legs fought to keep his body upright.

'It's the only way you'll ever make one,' said Lucy, as she continued to push him forwards.

Simon gingerly followed his friends across the water, gripping both guide ropes for support. The bridge started to sway under their combined weight, and all manner of groans and cracks echoed from the rotting structure.

'Why are you in such a rush, Lucy?' said Simon.

'That roll of film you found is all the

proof I needed. There's something hiding out here, and for the sake of your silly friends, I was rather hoping that we three *monster hunters* might just find it first.'

But their prey had found them first.

The sun vanished as a huge shadow fell across the trio. Whippet, Lucy and Simon stared up the river. A huge patch of darkness was blocking out the light. As they watched, the shadow extended a pair of wide wings and swooped across the water towards them at an incredible speed.

There was no escape, so Simon chose the only sensible course of action.

He shut his eyes!

CHAPTER 12

SPLASH!

'Hold on!' shouted Lucy, but her words were drowned out by an ear-piercing scream from the flying attacker. Simon's brain had just enough time to recognise the noise before the world turned upside down.

The dark mass blasted past them at a hundred miles an hour. One wing tip narrowly missed slicing Whippet's head from his shoulders.

But it did NOT miss the guide rope.

With a mighty *SNAP* the bridge plunged violently to one side, twisting as the remaining rope strained to hold the structure upright. Simon was dangling upside down, staring directly at the rushing water far below. His leg had caught in a loop of withered rope that was beginning to stretch and creak as he spun in a slow circle.

From his position Simon had a clear view up at the winged creature, as it circled around and prepared to charge them again.

And the camping trip had been going so well.

'*AGHHHH,*' screamed Simon.

'*AGHHHH,*' agreed Whippet, as he clung to a slippery plank. 'We're all going to die!'

'Nobody's going to die,' said Lucy, hanging beside Whippet, gripping on to the edge of a dangling plank by her right hand, 'but the next few minutes are going to be a little adventurous!'

Simon knew enough about their nine-year-old companion to understand what Lucy really meant by 'adventurous'. The next few minutes would most likely be filled with lots of screaming, shouting, perilous danger and life-passing-before-their-eyes moments. But Simon had begun to trust Lucy. She always had a plan – and of course that great rucksack of gadgets and weaponry.

Simon's trust disappeared in a heartbeat, however, when Lucy raised her machete high above her head with her free left hand. She was grinning. Lucy actually appeared to be enjoying herself.

'What are you doing?' asked Simon in horror.

'Saving our lives,' said Lucy, and with a wink she swung the machete and sliced through the final rope. The bridge fell apart just as the ball of darkness passed overhead.

Simon, Whippet and Lucy tumbled head over heels into the freezing river below like three pennies thrown into a wishing well. The shock of the cold water brought them rocketing back to the surface in seconds. Loose planks and sections of rope rained down around them as they fought to stay afloat. But the current was too strong. They were pulled further and further from the crossing point and the rest of the group standing in shock, high above on the bank.

They could see T-Rex shouting at them, but even his mighty voice was drowned by the noise of the river. A wave crashed over Simon's head and, for the first time since his meeting with the Snotticus, he realised he was scared. He was not a strong swimmer, and as he splashed desperately in the river

his wet clothes grew heavier and heavier.

Just as his arms and legs began to fail, he felt someone grip him around the neck.

'Hang on,' said Whippet, supporting Simon, 'I think I can get us to the shore!'

Unlike Simon, Whippet was a very good swimmer. He once claimed that he began doggy-paddling at the age of two, a fact that made complete sense, as the Willow family had been running a dog kennels since he was born.

But even so, the flow of water was just too powerful. Whippet's efforts had managed to slow them down but they were still stuck in the middle of the river.

'Hey – what's THAT?' panted Whippet, and Simon struggled to twist himself around. A flash of bright yellow was bouncing rapidly towards them from upriver.

'It's a rubber dinghy,' Simon shouted in relief.

The boat floated closer to the boys and a single paddle was thrust over the side. Whippet and Simon grabbed hold of it, pulled themselves up and tumbled into the bobbing yellow craft.

As they lay coughing and laughing with relief in the bottom of the boat, Simon realised that they had, once again, been rescued by a lunatic.

Lucy was standing above them in the dinghy, the paddle held proudly in one hand like a sword. She was soaking wet and her curly red hair was flying in the wind,

her cap now lost to the river. Simon was reminded again of the cover of **FEARLESS**, and the main character in *Red's Revenge*, the female warrior. Lucy was beginning to look more like that comic barbarian warrior every second!

'You packed an inflatable boat?' asked Simon as he struggled to sit up.

'Of course. I thought all you campers were taught to *be prepared*,' said Lucy.

Then she thrust the paddle back into the water and used it like a rudder, turning the dinghy sharply towards the riverbank. Simon's eyes widened when he realised what was about to happen next.

'Hold on,' said Lucy with a grin. 'This might be a little bumpy.'

CHAPTER 13

LOST ...
LIKE, *REALLY* LOST!

The little dinghy hit the shore with considerable force. The gnarled and twisted roots of an ancient willow tree growing on the bank tore through the rubber of the boat with a mighty *CRUNCH* and Lucy, Whippet and Simon were thrown from the raft. They crashed through the thick foliage of the forest before finally coming to rest in a heap.

'That's it,' said Whippet defiantly. 'That's the *last time* today that I pick myself up from the ground,' he continued, as he picked himself up from the ground.

Simon lay still among the fallen leaves and twigs and gingerly checked for broken bones. Everything seemed to be in one piece.

'T-Rex is going to be so mad,' said Whippet unhappily, wringing river water from his soaked top. 'That is, if he can ever find us.'

'Stop whining, Whippet. Things have worked out perfectly,' said Lucy, as she rummaged in her ever-resourceful backpack.

Whippet gave Lucy a long, hard stare,

then shook his head and began checking his pockets to make sure his precious sketch-book had not been lost. Amazingly, it was both safe and dry. Simon peered over Lucy's shoulder.

'I think I know what you mean,' he said. 'If there is something dangerous out here, it'll be much better that everyone else is far, far away.'

"T-Rex is a warrior but he's smarter than he looks,' said Lucy. 'I get the feeling he knew something like this would happen, possibly even secretly wanted it to happen. Testing us, drawing out the beast, who knows.'

Simon nodded slowly, remembering the fist-bump in the woods.

'So he knew you were *you* all along?' he said.

'Course. We go way back, but that's got

nothing to do with our mission.' She held aloft a circular device. 'We need to get our bearings so we can go *monster hunting!*'

The object had a cracked glass top and appeared to be leaking a large collection of cogs and bearings and other mechanical pieces.

'And what is *that* supposed to be?' said Whippet.

'It *was* a compass,' said Lucy with a huff. 'I must have landed on it when we crashed.'

'But . . . but that means . . . we're lost . . . like, *REALLY* lost,' said Whippet.

He took the shattered compass from Lucy and tried to stuff all the little broken parts back inside. It seemed to calm him down a little.

Simon spotted a tall tree nearby with plenty of handy branches.

'I've another solution to our problem. Give me a leg up, Lucy.'

Lucy cupped her hands and Simon used the foothold to boost himself into the lower branches of the tree. What Simon lacked in swimming skills he made up for with tree climbing. He was a superior scrambler and within minutes he had reached the top.

Simon's head broke through the upper canopy and, just as he'd hoped, he discovered he had a perfect view of the surrounding forest. He could see the river snaking away. Their rafting adventure had carried them a long way from the bridge crossing, and the waterway had curled around in a wide arc, dumping them on the opposite shore.

Simon craned his neck in all directions. He wanted to make sure he wasn't about to be ambushed by the flying horror. But there was nothing to be seen but trees and more trees and, a short distance away, an opening in the canopy. The trees thinned and Simon could just about make out some sort of structure, but it seemed to blend into the woodland.

'Hey, it looks like there's another camp up ahead. Perhaps they've got a phone,' he shouted.

'So what are we waiting for?' came Lucy's distant and rather rude reply from the ground.

What was Simon waiting for? He scanned the landscape beyond the new camp. His gaze settled on a hilltop that rose up above the canopy of the forest.

And there IT stood. All alone. A single pale tree trunk that reached high into the sky, like a skeletal finger. A black cloud hung above it, spitting forks of lightning like arrows from a bow.

Simon gulped as a familiar shiver tap-danced across his skin. He felt his story power rising, like the swell of a wave. Words floated up in his mind: *the boy with the magic chalk*. He swallowed, breathed in, let it break. The feeling passed.

These stories need an audience, thought Simon. *And they need to be told at the right time.*

This was not the moment. He scurried back down through the branches, smiling to himself. For the first time in weeks he began to believe in his ability to tell stories. Simon landed beside his friends in a crouch. Whippet was still fiddling ineptly with the compass.

'Leave that, Whippet. I know the way. Follow me,' he said, pointing in the direction of the new clearing, and the three of them plunged onwards into the undergrowth.

CHAPTER 14

TWITCHER HQ

Simon was the first to break through the wood and into the clearing. However his joy at finding the hidden camp instantly vanished as his feet became entangled in something, sending him flying headfirst into a muddy patch of earth.

'All that way through the forest without tripping once and the last root gets me,' he said, wiping dirt from his eyes as he pulled himself upright.

Lucy bent down and plucked something from the ground.

'It's not a root,' she said, waving a single red wellington boot.

Simon limped over and took the boot from her outstretched hand. Inside, written clearly in black marker pen, was the name *Nate Rumble*.

'Okay, that's weird,' said Whippet, as he and Simon stared at the mud-encrusted boot. 'How did it get all the way out here?'

'Let's find out,' said Lucy and she walked away towards the camp clearing.

It wasn't really much of a camp – just a single

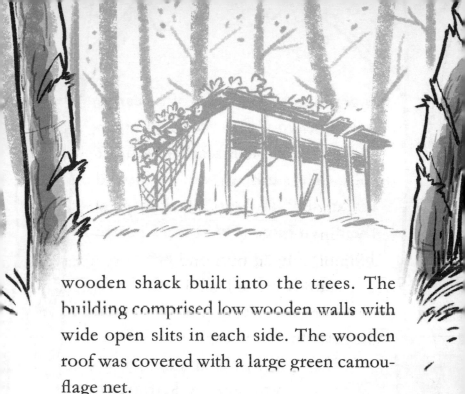

wooden shack built into the trees. The building comprised low wooden walls with wide open slits in each side. The wooden roof was covered with a large green camouflage net.

'And I thought our camp was in poor condition,' said Whippet. 'Look at this place. There are holes in all the walls!'

'It's meant to look like that,' said Simon.

'Yes. It's a hide,' agreed Lucy.

'What's it hiding from?' said Whippet, looking around nervously.

'Good question,' said Lucy, tracing her

fingers across the trunk of a nearby tree. The wood was scorched black and a great slashed scar had almost split the trunk in two. It looked remarkably similar to the damage at their own camp. Other trees nearby bore similar signs of violence.

'A hide is a sort of hut that bird-watchers use. To spot birds without disturbing them,' explained Simon.

'It's disturbing me,' said Whippet, who had walked around the side of the hut, while Lucy disappeared inside. Simon followed Whippet. Dozens of hand-painted messages had been daubed on the side in white paint, each more sensational than the last.

Keep Out! . . . Run, you fools! . . . Danger surrounds you! . . . Death is my neighbour! . . . If you can read this, you're

DOOOOOOOOOOOOMED!

'This looks like the entrance to your bedroom,' said Simon.

The boys heard a scrabbling sound from inside. As they entered the hide they saw that Lucy was rooting around on the floor. Books and photographs were scattered everywhere. It was a mess.

'That looks like a giant bird,' said Simon, picking up a random blurred picture from the floor.

'These snaps are so fuzzy that we could be looking at a butterfly, but taken together with the roll of film you found in the main camp, I'd say *this* is our monster,' said Lucy.

Lightning flashed. Thunder rolled, nearby and loud. Three, four hits in a row. Whippet grimaced.

'Seems like the birdwatchers left in a hurry. Where'd they go?' he said.

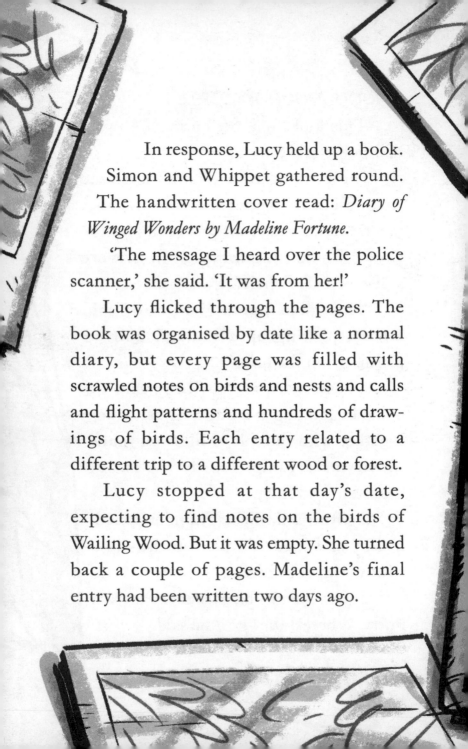

In response, Lucy held up a book. Simon and Whippet gathered round. The handwritten cover read: *Diary of Winged Wonders by Madeline Fortune.*

'The message I heard over the police scanner,' she said. 'It was from her!'

Lucy flicked through the pages. The book was organised by date like a normal diary, but every page was filled with scrawled notes on birds and nests and calls and flight patterns and hundreds of drawings of birds. Each entry related to a different trip to a different wood or forest.

Lucy stopped at that day's date, expecting to find notes on the birds of Wailing Wood. But it was empty. She turned back a couple of pages. Madeline's final entry had been written two days ago.

July 19th

My 'friends' ran away this afternoon. Finally I can get some peace! I didn't want to call the police from the main camp in the first place, but I never really believed anyone would come to investigate. The few who followed me to this hide soon showed their true colours. First they wrote those silly warnings (which I'll be painting over just as soon as I'm done) and then, when my flash bulb lit up the bird and they saw its true shape, they headed for the trees, screaming like their pants were on fire.

Good riddance, for this is the find of the century!

A NEW species! Appearing yesterday, from nowhere – and it's all mine. I won't share it with anyone. I shall call it the Aquila Fortuneos . . . my 'Lucky Eagle'. But my claim will mean nothing without a good photograph. I need proof. I need to get CLOSER!

'Fortune favours the bold,' Pappa used to say. I'm not sure how bold a milkman can be, but he had spirit.

And so now I go, and go boldly . . . into the belly of the beast . . .

A cool breeze whipped around their legs as the trio stood still. Lucy closed the book and popped it into her rucksack. 'Evidence,' she said to Simon. They walked back outside.

Simon stared up at the sky. The sunshine that had bravely fought its way through the forest canopy had been replaced, once more, by a sea of grey clouds. Lightning strikes came quicker than ever. The storm that had been threatening to break for two days appeared to be building.

The brooding sky perfectly reflected the mood of the group.

'I don't like the look of that,' whispered Whippet.

'You don't like much of anything,' said Lucy.

'That's not true – I like *drawing* and *comics*. But no, I don't like creepy hides filled with creepy pictures of a creepy beast and creepy warning messages.'

'Do you like Danica?' said Lucy.

Whippet's mouth opened and closed like a goldfish. *Pop pop.*

'She likes you. Don't ask me why,' said Lucy with a shrug.

Whippet's eyes danced left and right, as if his brain was playing table tennis with his pupils.

'But . . . but she *hates* me. She told me I should stand on my own two feet, and she told me weirdoes stuck together, and that I should ignore conspiracy theories and to

focus on what was right in front of me —
which was *her* at the time — and she said I
had a unique imagination . . . and she
touched my knee . . .'

Lucy gave Whippet a look.

'Is the penny dropping yet?'

'Oh . . .' said Whippet.

The penny had finally dropped.

Whippet smiled and blushed a dark
shade of ketchup.

'Girls,' said Lucy dismissively, as if she

wasn't really one herself.

'*Back* to the problem at hand,' said Simon. 'Before he went gaga, Whippet made a good point. I don't like this either. Last time we got dragged into the fight it was because my sister was in danger and we HAD to help out. But this is different. The birdwatchers were right to call the police. Someone might get hurt by this bird and right now that someone is likely to be one of *us*.'

Lucy waved one of the blurry photos under Simon's chin.

'What would you tell them? *Excuse me, officer, but I've just been attacked by a winged monster that I can't really describe and I've found a pile of old photos and a diary. Please send a squad car. It's urgent!*"

'Well, when you say it like that, and in *that* voice, then of course it sounds silly,' said Simon, but secretly he knew Lucy was right. His dad might have believed him, but without phone reception there was no way to even get him a message. Anyone else would simply think they were kids playing games.

Lucy glared from Simon to Whippet. She sighed.

'Okay, listen up,' said Lucy. 'You need to understand the scale of this thing.'

Simon folded his arms. *At last*, he thought. *Some answers!*

'I told you the monsters come from another world, and in a manner of speaking I was being truthful. They can't possibly have been created here on Earth. They are utterly unique.'

'What do you mean?' said Whippet. She had his full attention.

'Each monster is one of a kind.

Absolutely original. This bird . . . your *Snotticus* . . . each is as different as a snowflake. The twenty monsters I tracked and beat before them were the same. Unique.'

'So where do they come from? How are they getting here?' asked Simon.

Lucy bit her lip. 'Well, there's the comic connection . . . Eventually every one of these creatures makes an appearance in the pages of **FREAKY** or **FEARLESS**. But I don't know why. What I *do* know is that these monsters used to stay hidden in the town, they were nocturnal and never left Lake Shore. And they were extremely good at hiding. But the pattern has changed. They're taking risks now, moving in daylight, searching for something. It's hard to control them.'

Whippet squinted at Lucy, then broke out in a grin.

'Wait a minute . . . you're asking *us* to help *you!* Does the big bad explorer need two pathetic boys?'

Lucy grabbed Whippet by the shirt front and lifted him off the ground but she couldn't wipe the smile from his face.

'This is a once-in-a-lifetime offer, Chuckles – you want to join forces or not?' snarled Lucy.

'Will our new club have a name?' said Whippet as he dangled from her grip.

'No. No names.'

'We'll agree to disagree on that point. Anyway, I'm in,' replied Whippet, 'but only if I can design the club logo.'

'*No* names and *no* logos. But just make sure that there's a picture of a crossbow and a skull and a sword in there, okay? Now, what about *you*, Mossy?'

Simon stared at his best friend and his new friend. He thought about all the troubles behind them, and all the potential troubles to come. *Safety in numbers* . . . wasn't that what he'd said to Whippet?

'Me too,' he nodded. 'We won't get any closer to solving this mystery with a flying fiend on the loose. We'll stop it together. But first . . . I need to use the loo.'

CHAPTER 15

THE MOST
LIGHTNING-STRUCK
TREE IN THE WORLD

One quick trip behind a bush later and
Simon had rejoined his friends at the edge
of the clearing. Lucy and Whippet were
both wearing oversized wellingtons.

'Where did you find those?' asked Simon.

'Under another pile of photos inside,' said Lucy, throwing Simon his own pair. 'They're adult-sized and way too big, but that storm is going to break any second. I've been soaked enough for one day.'

'Okay, so now what?' said Whippet.

'Now *Simon* works his magic,' said Lucy.

'Ha! What are you talking about?' said Simon with a nervous laugh.

Lucy placed her hands on her hips.

'This might be a secret club, Simon, but we share our *own* secrets. Whippet and I have both seen your special skill in action. You're a STORY TELLER. So where does this story go next?'

A TELLER, thought Simon. That's what Captain Armstrong had said, back in the basement of his Shipshape Shop —

'. . . *one of the lads is a* TELLER . . .' He'd been talking about Simon. Despite the cold wind blowing through the camp, Simon felt a bead of sweat trickle down his neck.

'That's not how it works,' he said, 'and as I've been trying to explain, I can't just summon the power whenever I like. Why don't you ask Whippet? Maybe he could *draw* us a solution. A map that leads to the monster or something.'

'Hey, don't look at me,' said Whippet, holding up his hands in protest. 'I've no idea how this stuff works. I drew a mammoth. It came to life. But I've also drawn about a bazillion things that have NOT come to life!'

'Alright, alright, so there must be a trigger or something that sets you boys off,' said Lucy, turning away and folding her arms as she thought about the problem.

Simon realised he was still holding

Nate Rumble's wellington boot. An idea began to form.

'Maybe we haven't mastered our skills yet, but we can still use some common sense. If the birdwatchers didn't steal this welly, that only leaves our mystery monster. If it's pinching wellies and it dropped *one*, then maybe it's dropped some more.'

Lucy looked at Simon for a second then punched him on the arm, causing him to yelp. It wasn't a playful punch like Whippet might have delivered, but it was as close as Lucy got to saying, '*Smart thinking, Mossy.*'

The kids split up and searched the camp, scanning the ground. Whippet found the first one, a polka-dot boot standing upright, near some bushes that bordered the treeline. It belonged to Danica. Simon noticed that Whippet held on rather tightly to that one.

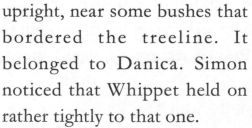

Lucy pushed through the foliage and scanned the open field beyond.

'There,' she shouted, spotting a blue and green striped welly lying on the ground.

The trio pushed through the bushes and they set off across a gradually rising plain, tracking the randomly scattered boots. The hill was a peculiar place. Simon noticed that not a single blade of green grew in the field, and what grass remained on the hillside was bone white.

Simon scuffed the ground as he walked.

'I wasn't *refusing* to use my power,' he said quietly.

'I know,' said Lucy.

'You do?' said Simon in surprise.

'Yup. Bet you've been trying to get it to work. Practising really, really hard, yeah?'

Simon nodded.

'This is not that sort of adventure,' said Lucy grimly. 'Take it from me, things never work out quite as you'd hope. Whatever set off your power is somehow connected to these monsters.'

'You think?'

'Yep. I'm only guessing, but for some reason I think they have to be close by for it to work.'

Simon chewed his lip.

'You know, Whippet actually *touched* the Snotticus,' said Simon. 'Well, it butted him in the bum.'

'Huh. Did you touch it too?' said Lucy.

'No,' replied Simon quickly. *But I did stroke that odd little creature, Gubbin*, he thought to himself. Fur like paper, flicking across his palm.

'That's interesting. Very interesting. And did Whippet high-five a monster right

before he drew his imaginary mammoth? The one that supposedly came to life?' said Lucy with a sarcastic grin.

'No, no, nothing like that. T-Rex just patted him on the shoulder.'

Lucy's grin disappeared, and she looked almost sad. But the expression vanished in an instant, replaced by a fierce snarl.

'Listen to me, this nonsense all started when you *met* the Snotticus, so if you boys want to learn how to use these powers, then I'm afraid you're going to have to put your-self in harm's way. Which is lucky, really, because that's where we're headed.'

The trio continued to trudge up the barren hill. Overhead, the lightning and thunder applauded their efforts

with strike after strike. It
was an eerie soundtrack to
their adventure.

'This place is REALLY spooky,'
said Whippet. 'Even the grass looks
scared to be here.'

'Can you blame it?' said Simon. Up
above an immense storm cloud was
swirling around a massive tree that

towered above them, standing alone on the crest of the hill. Simon was amazed. Once upon a time it must have been an absolutely mighty tree – vast, lush and proud – but now it resembled little more than a giant skeletal hand.

'What happened to the tree?' said Whippet.

'Struck by lightning. More than once probably, looking at this storm,' said Simon. 'The weather here is extreme.'

Lucy peered upwards, watching the dark clouds.

'Don't be soft. It's all because of the *bird*. It attracts the lightning . . . draws it in.'

'And *how* do you know it's up there?' said Simon, following her gaze.

'Because we've run out of dropped boots,' said Lucy, waving a solitary white boot that had been lying against the base of the trunk, 'and the only direction left to explore . . . is UP!'

'Could be a trap,' said Whippet nervously.

Lucy shrugged and pulled a long length of rope from her backpack, slung it over her left shoulder, then attached a round black disc to the palm of each hand. She flexed her fingers.

'*Explorer-class Climbing Pads*. My own design. Can cling to any surface. Unfortunately, I've only got one pair, so you two will have to follow me up by rope.'

Simon and Whippet watched in silence as Lucy pulled herself up the side of the tree, attaching and releasing one sucker at a time. The further she climbed the more she looked like a tiny insect scaling a flower. It really was a huge tree.

'She doesn't even care that the monster might be waiting for us, luring us in. These wellies, all laid out in a neat row for us to find – it's just too easy. I know I say this a lot,' whispered Whippet, turning to Simon, 'but Lucy really is quite mad.'

Whippet groaned as a large length of rope hit him in the head.

'*Quite* mad . . . but a *very* good shot,' came the tiny voice from high above them. 'Now get up here. I've found our intrepid twitcher.'

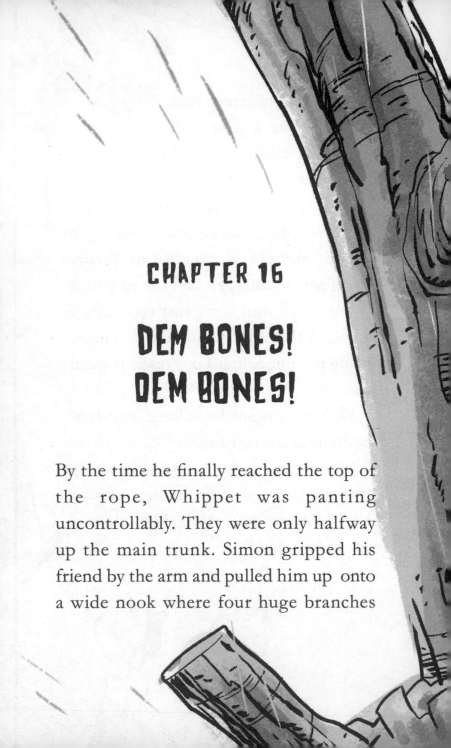

CHAPTER 16

DEM BONES!
DEM BONES!

By the time he finally reached the top of the rope, Whippet was panting uncontrollably. They were only halfway up the main trunk. Simon gripped his friend by the arm and pulled him up onto a wide nook where four huge branches came together to form a sort of platform.

'How did . . . *puff* . . . Lucy make . . . *wheeze* . . . that look so EASY?'

'Well, she wasn't carrying a girl's welly in one hand,' said Simon, noting that Whippet was still clutching Danica's boot.

His friend did his best to ignore him.

'Never again. I'm not following her again! That climb nearly killed me,' said Whippet as he fought to regain his breath. What little air he'd managed to suck into his lungs burst out when he discovered his face was centimetres from the

grinning teeth of a human SKULL!

Now, Whippet knew what a skeleton was. Every issue of **FREAKY** featured piles of rotting corpses because, well, because they were cool. Even their school science laboratory had a life-sized plastic skeleton, nicknamed Mr Jangles, who hung in the corner of the room. Skeletons were fun. The slumped heap of bones lying before his wide eyes, however, was *not* in the least bit amusing. This was the REAL thing. Whippet scrabbled

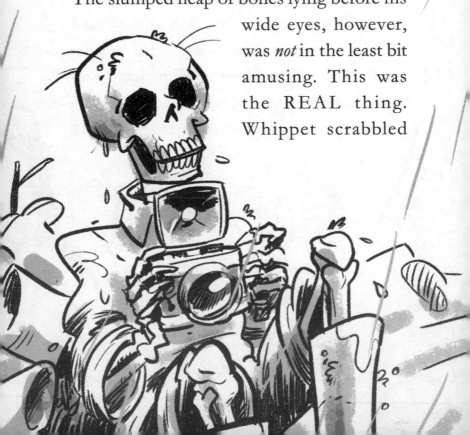

frantically backwards across the branches in his attempt to get away, tripped, and fell onto something soft.

Simon was still looking at the skeleton. He took a tentative step closer. The figure was clutching an old-fashioned camera to its chest, complete with a flash-bulb mounted on top. Simon peered at it. Four words had been etched into the metal. *Property of M. Fortune.*

'It's her,' said Simon, fighting to control his panic. 'Madeline Fortune! She's dead!'

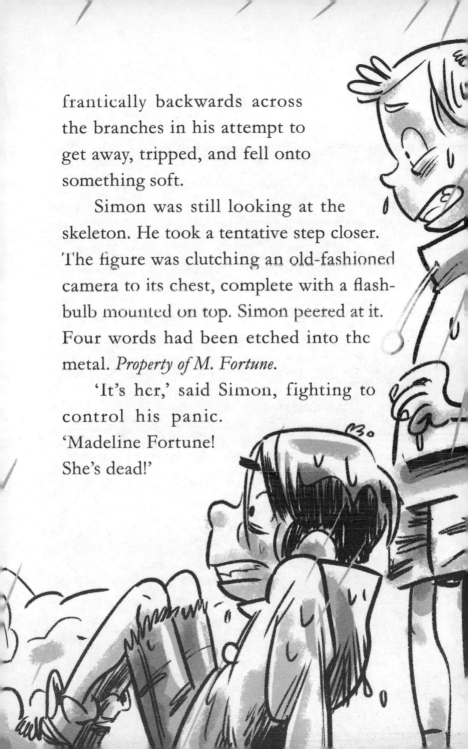

'Observant as ever,' said Lucy.

'But according to her journal she was alive only *yesterday!* Aren't bodies supposed to be a bit more . . . er . . . *gooey* when they're fresh?' said Simon.

'Yeah,' said Whippet, 'and why is she halfway up a tree, lying beside a nest made of wellies?'

Simon wrinkled his brow then looked at his friend. Somehow, Simon had failed to notice that a large portion of the branch platform onto which they had climbed was, in fact, occupied by a bird's nest. A nest made entirely from rubber boots, into which Whippet had just fallen.

'You're inside a nest of wellies,' said Simon.

'Observant as ever,' repeated Lucy, but

she couldn't quite remove the surprise from her own voice.

'This is where our wellies went,' said Whippet, waving Danica's boot in one hand, 'but why diiii*mmphh!*'

'Shhhhh . . .' Lucy whispered, clamping a hand firmly over Whippet's mouth and pointing to the edge of the nearby forest.

Hanging over the woodland was a large bank of cloud. As they watched, a small slice of the cloud seemed to break away and swoop directly towards them. The ball of cloud swept past at an impossible speed, spiralling up and around the tree, leaving a trail of sparks in its electrical wake.

'The monster,' whispered Whippet.

Lucy growled.

'Attacked us on the bridge, disintegrated the toilet, almost fried Nate, ripped up two camps, stole our wellies, terrorised the twitchers and skeletonised poor old Madeline Fortune,' she said.

With a *THUMP* that rattled the teeth in their heads, the mysterious creature came to rest far above them, on the highest branch of the tree.

'This thing has to be stopped,' said Lucy.

Feathers, thought Simon, as he stared upwards. So many white feathers. And claws. It was a horrifying tangle of wings and talons and danger. His sense of fear began to rise, and with it came the familiar tingle, the tickle of book pages brushing his skin. He blinked.

Was Lucy right? Was this how it worked? Was his power activated only when he came face to face with a monster and was terrified out of his mind? That would be cruel but . . . but . . .

But I am a TELLER.

Captain Armstrong knew it and now, so did Simon.

'What's a TELLER?' whispered Lucy, then she spun away as the beast screeched high above, twisting its head to and fro. It stretched its impossibly wide wings and gave them a single thunderous flap. It was a monstrous thing.

And then a bolt of lightning hit it.

Actually hit it, right on the head.

The monster unleashed a glass-shattering scream from its gaping mouth, a mouth like a miniature black hole. A burst of lightning erupted from the monster's

mouth, spiralling off into the sky.

Whippet and Lucy jumped, but Simon just smiled peacefully. To Simon, everything seemed so calm.

He was a TELLER.

Poor old Madeline wasn't. *She might have been good at watching birds*, thought Simon, *but she was terrible at naming them*. Simon wasn't. This was the one and only *Screaming Haggle*. Obviously.

The bird flapped its huge wings and took to the skies once more.

'Screaming Haggle?' said Whippet thoughtfully. 'Yeah . . . that sounds about right, Mossy. Almost better than the Snotticus.'

Simon had been speaking out loud again.

'I don't care what it's called, I just care where it went,' said Lucy.

Simon sensed the real world rushing in on him again, but this time he retained a little of his calm. The power hadn't completely left him. It felt like it was just waiting for the right moment.

He looked around. The Screaming Haggle really had disappeared.

'Oh boy,' said Whippet with a little whimper.

Lucy slowly slid her backpack from her shoulders. She was just about to dip her hand inside – possibly, Simon hoped, to retrieve a gold-plated Haggle harpoon gun – when a blur of sparks and feathers and noise whipped through the tree branches and knocked her rucksack out of her hand.

As they watched in misery, Lucy's magical bag of tricks sailed through the air and came to rest on the ground far below with an expensive thump. The Haggle flew away from them again, sparks showering from its feathers, and then turned in the air to survey its domain with fiery eyes.

'We're dead . . . we're DEAD,' howled Whippet.

'The day a budgie gets the better of me is the day I quit hunting monsters,' said Lucy with determination. Then she gripped a nearby branch and, using her sucker pads, began to climb upwards like a monkey.

'What are you doing? You can't beat that beast with your bare hands,' said Simon, staring after her.

'I'm going to buy you time to come up with a real plan – and it had better be good! Prove you're worthy of your newfound powers, boys!'

Lucy disappeared. A lightning bolt hit the Haggle in midair and the monster bellowed another tree-shaking scream, a stream of sparks blasting forth from its mouth.

An idea began to take shape in Simon's mind.

'Grab your pencils, Whippet,' said Simon. 'I think there's a way to beat this thing . . . but there might be one *tiny* snag . . .'

CHAPTER 17

THE GREAT DRAW-OFF

As the boys bent over their frantically drawn battle plan, laid out on pages torn from Whippet's sketchbook, they became aware that Simon's scheme contained more than just *one* tiny snag. In fact, according to Whippet's evaluation, Simon's plan was made up entirely of snags.

'Can we go over this again?' said

Whippet, as the sound of fireworks and roars echoed high above them, accompanied by a small voice shouting, '*Even I can fly better than that, you big feathered NIT!*'

'Sure,' said Simon.

'If we can lure the Haggle into the tree, and if we can somehow find a way to stop it from escaping, then there's a tiny chance that it might be destroyed if it's hit *directly* by a lightning bolt,' said Whippet.

'Exactly,' said Simon.

Whippet scratched his head with his pencil.

'But Lucy said it already attracts lightning.'

'You've heard it scream,' said Simon. 'I don't think it likes the lightning at all. This storm has been buzzing over the forest since we got here. It's following the bird wherever it goes, zapping it constantly. And we all just saw what happens when it gets struck. It can't contain it. It has to get rid of it or it might go *BANG!* This nest is the proof.'

Whippet looked at the wellington boots.

'What do you mean?' he said.

'Rubber insulates against electricity. That's why the Haggle stole all our boots and built a nest from them. It's been trying to protect itself,' said Simon. 'If we can trap it here, outside the nest, then the lightning should be able to overpower it. The bird won't be able to run or hide from all the strikes.'

Whippet looked uncertain.

'It's a gamble, sure, but it's the best chance we've got,' said Simon.

Whippet pulled at his hair.

'You really think the lightning might

destroy it?' he said.

'I almost feel sorry for the monster, but we're out of options,' said Simon.

'Sure, but how can we even lure it down here? What's it drawn to? Why did it attack the twitchers?'

Simon smiled then reached over and pulled the camera from the skeletal hands of Madeline Fortune. In doing so, her head became dislodged and fell off. Both boys shivered at the sight of the skull rolling around the nest. Simon held up the camera.

'Flashbulbs. That's what the Haggle saw. All those birdwatchers snapping pictures must have looked like they were firing off little bolts of lightning. That would have driven the bird crazy. And when Nate was zapped in the toilet, he'd been waving T-Rex's torch around. Same thing . . .'

Simon ran the whole idea back through

his mind again, checking the logic. It all hung together, but it didn't explain why the Haggle had attacked them on the bridge. Why had it come for them?

Another scream exploded overhead. The boys did not have long.

'Okay, so you use that camera to get it down here, then what, Mossy? We can't stop the Haggle from simply flying away again!'

'Ah, that's where you come in,' said Simon with a smile.

'Huh? Me?'

'Don't think, buddy. Clear your mind. Don't concentrate on anything at all, just pick up your pencil and show me how YOU would stop a monster in its tracks. Draw us a solution.'

Whippet frowned, then shrugged and

started to scribble. He was feeling panicked and nervous and excited and he wasn't thinking . . . which was exactly what Simon wanted. Yesterday morning, when they'd arrived at the camp and Whippet had drawn a woolly mammoth wearing a bandana, he had not been thinking about anything in particular. T-Rex had clapped him hard on the shoulder and in his dazed state he'd just drawn his heart out. Maybe NOT thinking was part of the key to unlocking *Whippet's* ability, mused Simon.

Either way, it was worth a shot. It worked once, but would it work *again*?

Whippet's pencil danced across the page, guided by only the most basic part of his brain.

'I guess your classic solution would be to use an industrial-sized tub of glue. Cartoon style. Some sort of crazy-sticky stuff. The kind of gloop that could halt a charging wildebeest . . .'

The world shifted slightly. Whippet's pencil took on a life of its own, blurring in the boy's hand as it skittered and jumped across his sketchpad. Whippet's eyes glazed and he *drewanddrewanddrew*.

Finally he stopped, and sat, panting from his efforts.

There was a RIPPING sound. The air stretched around them like a swollen balloon. It was the same sound and the

same sensation that Simon had heard the previous day when Whippet drew the mammoth. And just like that, Simon's understanding of how the world worked disintegrated all over again.

He looked slowly from the sketch held in
Whippet's hand to the blue cylindrical item
that his best friend was sitting on. It was a
large tin labelled: *Gloop! The Super-Sticky
Stuff.* It looked like a prop ripped from a
cartoon.

'It worked . . . it really worked,' whispered Simon slowly.

Whippet looked down at the pad in front of him. Then he stared at the tin between his legs.

'Okay,' said Whippet as he stood up. 'Consider me officially freaked out.'

Simon took the sketchbook from Whippet's hand, picked up the tin, and held the two identical items side by side. Bizarrely, they didn't just look the same, they felt the same. The tin felt like paper, which was odd, but not as odd as the fact it existed at all!

Simon grinned at his best friend.

'You wanted a superpower, Whippet? Well, you've got one.'

Just then, Lucy – her hair smoking and her clothes significantly singed – slid down a branch at full speed and landed in a crouch between them. She patted a small flame on her sleeve as if it were nothing more irritating than a fly.

'What exactly have you been *doing* up there?' said Simon. 'How did you keep that monster busy?'

'Trade secret, Mossy, but it involved jumping from branch to branch like a monkey and insulting the bird. A lot. I certainly got its attention, as it swooped down at me over and over, but it just wouldn't attack!'

Simon held up Madeline's camera. He gave the flashbulb a flick.

'It will in about a second so you'd better take cover!'

And with that Simon raised the camera to the sky and began to snap pictures, spinning on the spot. *Flash. Flash. Flash. Flash. Flash.* The tree lit up. Then the sky lit up.

Then the Screaming Haggle came in for the kill.

'Here we go!' yelled Lucy as she and Whippet dived into the nest of wellies.

The Haggle swept towards the tree. At the last minute it gave a huge flap of its wings and came to a stop, hovering in the air just outside Simon's reach. Streams of hot sparks flickered across its feathers. It beat its huge wings and screamed.

'Where's Simon?' said Lucy, discovering that their hiding place was one friend short.

Whippet popped his head over the nest.

'I do believe Mossy is having a go at being brave.'

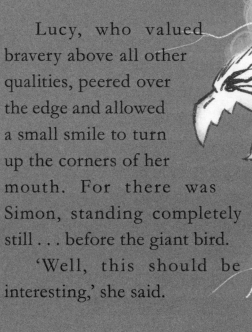

Lucy, who valued
bravery above all other
qualities, peered over
the edge and allowed
a small smile to turn
up the corners of her
mouth. For there was
Simon, standing completely
still . . . before the giant bird.

'Well, this should be
interesting,' she said.

CHAPTER 18

EVERYTHING COMES UNSTUCK

'Mr Bird, it doesn't have to end like this,' said Simon, waving the camera above his head. 'I'd have gone a little crazy if I'd been zapped by lightning every day, but you have to change your ways! What do you say?'

The Haggle cocked its head to one side

and peered around the platform. It seemed to be looking for a trap. Then all of a sudden it made up its mind and dived towards Simon at such speed that he nearly forgot to leap aside – at the very last moment.

Simon bundled into his friends, sending them sprawling across the nest as the Haggle crashed into the branches in the exact spot Simon had been standing. The impact of the creature shook the tree.

'*Gotcha!*' yelled Simon.

The Haggle struggled to pick itself up, only to discover that it could not. Whippet's puzzlement turned to celebration as he saw the upturned tin of *Gloop!* glue lying before the monster. Simon had been balancing on tiptoes on top of the can, while its contents had slowly seeped across the branches.

The Haggle was trapped.

'Yeah!' shouted Whippet in delight as

the first sparks of electricity zipped through the sky and crackled around them.

'I think we're about to be joined by some lightning,' said Simon.

'So what's our escape strategy?' said Lucy.

Whippet picked up their scribbled battle plan.

'We're supposed to be a long way from here! Look, I drew us back at the camp, smiling and drinking hot chocolate. We look really happy.'

'Back at camp . . . right . . . so, *NOT* standing in the tree with the monster?' said Lucy.

'Um . . . no. Definitely not,' said Whippet.

Lucy turned to Simon, who shook his head.

'Sorry, guys. We can't risk the Haggle breaking free,' said Simon. 'We need to be here till the very end, so you'd better cover

yourself in rubber boots – we'll need all the insulation from the electricity we can get. Let's just hope this works!'

Which of course it didn't.

The first lightning bolt struck the tree with a force that rattled their teeth. It leaped from branch to branch then hit the Haggle in the head, drawn to the monster like iron fillings to a magnet. The monster let out a bellow, its mouth stretched open and it expelled the lightning, firing the bolt directly at the trio who were cowering in their rubber shelter.

Boots were tossed in all directions but the wellies surrounding the children soaked up the energy, saving them from the deadly blast. The Haggle continued to wrench itself from side to side, fighting and struggling to break free.

'Well, we definitely just found out what happened to Madeline! It can use the lighting as a *weapon!* She must have taken a direct hit and been fried, instantly,' yelped Whippet, as he scurried across to rejoin his friends on all fours, boots on both his feet and his hands.

'I really hoped the electricity would stun it,' said Simon miserably, 'but the Haggle's *never* going to stop. The nest won't survive those blasts and we'll be destroyed long before it grows tired of fighting!'

Lucy fumed. She stared at the screaming monster. She stared at the skeleton of Madeline Fortune. Then she grabbed Simon by the shoulder.

'We're going to have to permanently shut that fiend's gob! But in order to do *that* I need it sitting nice and still with its mouth OPEN.'

'*We are toast, we are toast . . .*' said Whippet with a whimper.

'Not yet,' said Lucy, never taking her eyes off Simon. 'Do your thing, Fearless, and do it well. If you don't, our story ends right here.'

It wasn't a request. It wasn't polite. It was a life or death situation.

He was a TELLER. And it was time to get to work.

Simon rose from the nest and calmly strolled out to face the monster. Whippet reached out to stop him but he lightly shrugged his friend off with a kind smile. Standing before the vision of feathers and fury, Simon nodded. He didn't need a prop. He didn't need to find something to inspire a story, because the bird itself could be the story.

Nate Rumble was a bit of a bully, but he

hadn't *always* been . . . and perhaps the same might once have been said about the Haggle . . .

A Feathered Friend

A long, long time ago, in the days of yore, there was a rather unfortunate kingdom called Scuzzy. The people of Scuzzy didn't like the name, but all the good names had been taken, so that was that.

Anyway, in the kingdom there lived a tailor. He was called Flob, which was the only name worse than Scuzzy, and all the citizens made sure he knew it. They laughed at him. A lot. His name was silly and the clothes he made were rubbish. Really, really bad.

One day, when he was tired of

children pointing and laughing at him, and tired of having bedpans 'accidentally' tipped on him from open windows, Flob headed for the great forest. He didn't have a friend in the world and just wanted to be alone with his misery, but like every other miserable wish he'd ever made in his miserable life, it was not to be granted.

Without warning a giant bird dropped

from the branch of a nearby tree and settled on the ground before him. Flob nearly wet his poorly sewn pants, and who could blame him, for the bird was huge and very unusual. It was covered from beak to tail tip in long bone-white feathers, feathers so wide and silky that they seemed to sparkle with power.

Flob looked from his dreary clothes to the bird's feathers and an idea began to form. Summoning every drop of courage – which took about a second – Flob asked the bird for a single feather.

The beast cooed, and shook loose two bright white feathers. Flob thanked the

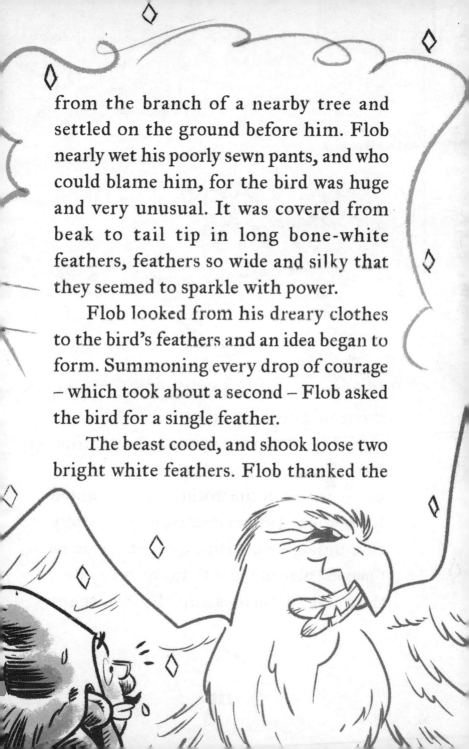

bird, then sprinted back to Scuzzy. All
night he sewed and stitched in his little
workshop, and when the sun finally rose,
he marvelled at his creation. A waistcoat
so white, so bright, that it lit up the room.
Flob slipped it on and walked proudly
through the streets. Street urchins
opened their mouths to make rude jokes,
then closed them again. Full bedpans

hovered . . . but were *NOT* emptied on Flob's head.

His waistcoat changed everything.

Word spread and before long Flob was kneeling before the Queen of Scuzzy. She wished for a dress of that same glistening material, so Flob headed back to the forest. He was fearful that the bird might not be there, or worse . . . that it wouldn't share another feather with him. Yet it was, and it did. For the bird believed Flob to be a friend. A true friend.

It could not have been *more* wrong. Flob was in it for the cash, and the Queen was in it for all she could get. Not content with a single dress, she ordered bedspreads, tablecloths, underwear, overwear, tupperware . . . That everything be made from the white feathers. And as Flob granted her wishes, his wealth and reputation grew . . . and so did his greed.

Finally the Haggle realised that Flob was not a friend. The fact that it was down to its last feather and looked like a bald pink turkey should have been a clue, but it was a simple beast.

Just not a forgiving one.

And so, as Flob stretched out his hand to claim the final feather, the once-peaceful bird exacted its brutal revenge.

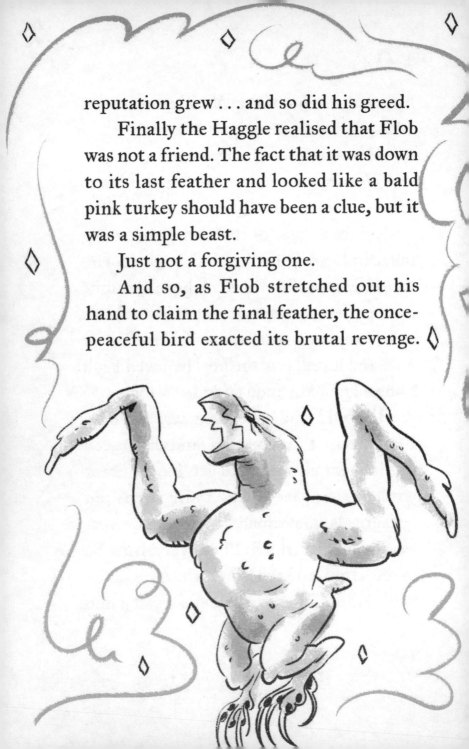

With a scream of fury it streched its neck towards Flob, its beak wide open.

No. Wider.

Wider . . .

'Perfect!' yelled Lucy.

Simon looked up. The Screaming Haggle was frozen in place before him – his storytelling power had worked its crazy magic. And this time, following his commands, the monster's mouth was wide open. It had done exactly what he'd asked – on Lucy's orders – and Simon was amazed.

In the precious seconds before the bird broke free of the spell, Lucy hurled something white and round directly into its beak, where it lodged solid. Then she grabbed Simon and dragged him back to the nest.

'What did you just do?' asked Simon.

'Gave Madeline Fortune a proper send-off,' said Lucy.

Simon stared at the Haggle. There, wedged in its mouth, like a giant gobstopper, stuck fast with a thick coating of *Gloop!* glue ... was a human skull.

And, like all skulls, it was grinning.

CHAPTER 19

T-REX TO THE RESCUE

As Simon, Whippet and Lucy scrabbled to turn the shattered nest into a new protective igloo, a mind-meltingly huge bolt of energy struck the tree. The bolt forked into the Haggle and the bird began to twitch and shudder violently as the boundless electricity built up inside its body. This time there would be no release, for the Haggle's

beak was stuck fast and stoppered.
It couldn't expel the electric
energy. There was only one
possible outcome.

Simon closed his eyes.

KA-
BOOOOOOOOOO-
OOOOOOM!

The tree was ripped apart by the force of the explosion, turned into matchsticks, and the nest and its contents were thrown into the air.

The trio tumbled in freefall. Simon did *not* see his life pass before his eyes. He did however see a lot of rubber boots. He was just thinking how sad it was that he'd survived meeting another monster and being electrocuted only to perish from a mighty fall, when his descent came to an end in a most unusual way.

He was caught.

By T-Rex.

The camp leader appeared to be riding on the back of a woolly mammoth. Whippet's woolly mammoth, to be precise. T-Rex had caught Simon like a Frisbee.

'Er . . .' said Simon. It was really all he had left.

'No time explain. Other kids need catching,' said T-Rex, and the mammoth bounded off, first to the right so T-Rex could snag Lucy, then to the left to grab Whippet, who appeared to be clutching a single welly like his life depended on it. And all the while, the mammoth narrowly dodged a rainstorm of branches and woodchips.

Against the odds they made it across the barren plain to the trees in one piece. The mammoth slowed gradually to a trot. Then it stopped. T-Rex lowered them one by one, then dropped to the ground beside them.

No one spoke for what seemed like an age.

Then Whippet turned to the others, held up one palm, face down, and wiggled his fingers.

'So *that's* how they run.'

Simon and Lucy burst into laughter. You had to hand it to their friend – Whippet's timing was good. Their camp leader and saviour watched them laugh, allowing them to release all the stress of the day. Then he held up a thick finger.

'Six-legged mammoth not belong here. T-Rex take mammoth somewhere safe, after T-Rex take kids home.'

'Where's everyone else?' said Simon.

'Packing bus. Good friend keep them safe.'

Although they had a million questions for their camp leader, T-Rex refused to answer a single one, telling them he was already in enough trouble for letting them out of his sight and putting them in harm's way. According to T-Rex, there would be a time for answers soon enough, but that was someone else's responsibility. He then walked them back through the forest in silence, stopping only twice. Firstly, at a secluded spot in the heart of the wood, to tether the mammoth (by its own bandana) to an oak tree. The animal happily obeyed his commands and settled down to munch lazily on the nearby foliage. As the others made ready to set off again, Whippet stole away from the group and gingerly approached the beast.

'Thanks for the catch, buddy,' he whispered quietly, before giving one of the mammoth's furry legs a farewell hug. 'I'd always had a feeling that one day art would save my life, and you did.'

The second stop was right outside the camp clearing. T-Rex turned and handed Lucy a cap. It was imprinted with the words *Wailing Wood*.

'Lucy need new disguise?'

Lucy paused, looked at the cap, then shook her head.

'No more hiding. No more secrets. No more disguises. Ever,' she said, looking at Simon and Whippet in turn.

Had he always *known that Joe was Lucy?* wondered Simon. Then the four of them stepped out from the trees and into the arms of the rest of the group, where twenty excitable faces and a thousand impossible questions awaited. Including a lot of 'who are YOU?'s directed at Lucy.

Only one member of the camp party, the 'good friend' T-Rex had mentioned, did not ask them about their adventure. Standing quietly to one side, Captain Armstrong appeared content to watch. Then, unseen by all but the intrepid trio, he slowly raised his hand and gave them a smart salute.

Simon felt his heart soar.

That small gesture almost made the madness of the day worthwhile.

CHAPTER 20

BACK TO THE BACK OF THE BUS

The return to town was a quiet affair. After the initial excitement died down the group had concentrated on packing the van, and then the realisation that their trip was over sank in. Scenery passed with little comment. Simon mentally ran through some of the important things that were *not* being said by his best friends.

1) 'Hey, Captain Armstrong, we just survived a battle with a Haggle and I've a feeling you knew it was coming . . . spill the beans!'

2) 'Mr Recks, where did you learn to ride a mammoth?'

3) 'Er . . . are we going to have to pay for the tree we just blew up?'

But, slightly less important things *had* been said. Not long after they'd set off, Nate had sidled sheepishly up to Whippet, provoking a fit of giggles from the other kids. But for once the laughs weren't aimed at Whippet. Nate's hair would never recover from his electrically charged encounter with the Haggle. It stood on end like a field of wheat and try as he might Nate just couldn't pat it down.

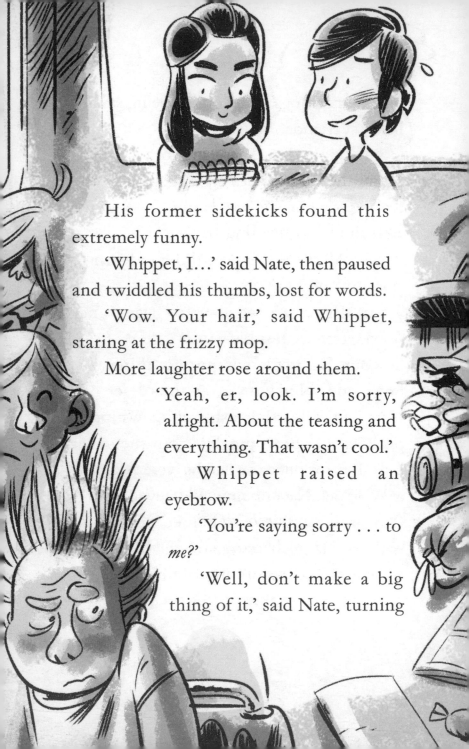

His former sidekicks found this extremely funny.

'Whippet, I…' said Nate, then paused and twiddled his thumbs, lost for words.

'Wow. Your hair,' said Whippet, staring at the frizzy mop.

More laughter rose around them.

'Yeah, er, look. I'm sorry, alright. About the teasing and everything. That wasn't cool.'

Whippet raised an eyebrow.

'You're saying sorry . . . to *me?*'

'Well, don't make a big thing of it,' said Nate, turning

in a huff and heading back to his seat.

It wasn't a classic apology, thought Simon, but it would do. Whippet was making new friends. The girl sitting beside him was further proof of that.

Danica leafed through Whippet's sketchbook and stopped at the woolly mammoth again. She traced a finger around the ketchup-stained bandana.

'Better with red, right?'

'Better with red,' said Whippet nervously. He wasn't used to sharing his comic art with anyone except Simon.

'Oh, I've got you something,' said Whippet suddenly, bending down to open his rucksack. Danica's eyes widened as he pulled out a single solitary polka-dot wellington boot. It was a little charred and melted but still recognisable as her boot.

'Sorry, I couldn't find the other one –' began Whippet but was cut off in mid-sentence by Danica, as she threw her arms around him for a lingering hug.

'Thank you, Whippet,' she said softly, after finally letting him go. 'You really are one of a kind.'

Whippet couldn't think of a reply to that.

'Now, are you aware,' Simon heard her continue, in a louder voice, 'that there is a readers' art competition in **FREAKY** at the moment? You should enter your mammoth . . .'

Simon turned to Lucy. While they were together, he wanted to get a few things straight. Lucy had decided to join them on the bus for the return trip. Whippet had tried to ask her where she'd found the limousine that had delivered her to camp in the first place, but she'd ignored the question.

'Sorry about your rucksack,' Simon began, working his way up to the big stuff.

'I'm not. It's just full of tools. They're replaceable, unlike you two.'

Simon grinned. Compliments from Lucy were extremely rare and needed to be enjoyed while they lasted.

'He *drew* the glue? He really drew it? And the mammoth?' said Lucy in a whisper.

Simon nodded and Lucy leaned back in her seat.

'Huh. Well, that is something. And

you're a TELLER, Simon. You change the way people and creatures act, with your *words*. As Whippet seems to be giving new meaning to the expression *life-like art* . . . I guess that makes him a CREATOR.'

'I guess. And that's pretty cool and everything, but . . . where does this end?' said Simon. 'We're both just making it up as we go along. We've been lucky so far, but I'm scared that sooner or later that luck's going to run out.'

Lucy cracked her knuckles.

'Agreed. And that's why we're going to track down the source of these creatures.'

'Where would we even begin?' said Whippet, rejoining the conversation while Danica happily flipped through his sketchbook.

Lucy stood up. She adjusted her cap then turned to Simon and Whippet.

'Lake Shore is the key. Like I said, these

monsters don't leave the town. The far edge of Wailing Wood marks the furthest boundary on the map. *Something* is holding them here. The town is connected. **FREAKY** and **FEARLESS** are connected. T-Rex and Captain Armstrong too. They both know more than they're prepared, or allowed, to say. I've tried turning the thumbscrews, believe me.'

Simon grimaced. He did believe her. Lucy was not your average investigator. She was more likely to swing an axe than ask a question. Which is exactly what Red, the **FEARLESS** comic warrior maiden, would do, he thought.

'But we're still missing a piece of the puzzle. We find that piece and we put the whole thing together. And then we stop it. Stop it so it STAYS stopped, got it?'

'Stop it. Got it,' said the boys in unison.

Lucy gave a tiny smile.

'You two idiots are alright, y'know?' she said, strolling down the aisle. Simon felt the bus slow to a halt. Lucy bumped knuckles one last time with T-Rex, and nodded to Captain Armstrong, then jogged down the stairs and away.

Whippet chewed on his pencil.

'You have to hand it to Lucy, she's a dedicated little nutcase,' he said. 'Resourceful too. Where *did* she get that limousine? If you ask me, we're missing a key piece of *her* puzzle.'

Simon was kneeling on his seat and looking out the rear window. He wanted to wave goodbye to Lucy but instead he grabbed Whippet by the collar and yanked him upwards.

'How's *that* for a solution?' he asked in wonder.

Lucy Shufflebottom, master of disguise, action heroine, explorer extraordinaire, good friend and vanquisher of monsters was opening the wrought-iron gates that led to Castle Fearless. The headquarters for the **FEARLESS** comic. As they stared

open-mouthed, Lucy walked through the gates and headed up the driveway, comic in hand. She walked as if she owned the place.

And perhaps, pondered Simon as the bus pulled away, she did.

Lucy heard the bus drive away and she stopped walking. She stood in the driveway and stared at the comic. Something was niggling at the back of Lucy's mind. She quickly flipped through the pages until she found the right story . . .

FREAKY
ISSUE #2168
HORROR WAITS IN THE CASTLE OF FEAR!
INSIDE: IGOR'S REVENGE!

Lucy slowly lowered the comic. She hadn't moved from her spot on the driveway. The small, strange creature known as Gubbin had watched the bus leave, and stayed there, sitting upon the gravel beside his red-haired friend as she turned the pages. Gubbin was used to staying still and keeping quiet. Where he came from, it was a vital survival tactic.

Lucy chewed on the inside of her mouth. She closed the comic and looked at the cover. It was the latest edition.

There was the Screaming Haggle . . . right there in the pages of **FREAKY**.

The comics. The town. The monsters. Lucy ran the mystery around her head but it was like building a jigsaw only to discover halfway through that instead of jigsaw pieces you'd actually been given bars of soap. Or fish. Or jelly. It didn't work. First the Snotticus and now the Screaming Haggle had made an appearance in the two most popular comics in town. Monsters they had fought for real had been included in made-up stories.

How was that possible? Who was

responsible? Lucy's list of suspects was extremely small. She did not like the thought of where her own story was headed. For it was T-Rex, her friend, who had clapped Whippet on the shoulder, after which the silly boy had gone and drawn a mammoth. A mammoth that came to life.

Lucy sighed.

Nobody was quite who they claimed to be. Except, perhaps, Simon and Whippet.

'Pfft . . . you know, Gubbin, we may have our work cut out with those two,' she said, 'but they have potential.'

Then they turned and began the long walk up the drive towards Castle Fearless.

High above them, on an upper castle floor, a curtain twitched beneath the fingers of an old hand.

'You know, we may have our work cut out with those two,' said a voice.

There was a grunt from behind.

'Lucy and her pet?'

The question came from a tired-looking man sitting in a plush leather chair.

'No, the boys! They seem to have a surprising knack for erasing our escapees. I'm grateful for their help, obviously, but their meddling might eventually lead them *here* . . . perhaps it is inevitable.'

The man in the chair turned slowly to look at his companion. His brow was furrowed.

'What are you suggesting?'

The man by the window thought for a moment, then snapped his fingers.

'That's it! I'll invite them. How could they possibly say no? Castle Fearless is the grand home of comics! True, it will be a terrible sacrifice, but a necessary one. We must protect our monstrous secret.'

The other man growled. 'WE are the monsters. You and I. If it wasn't for the girl…'

'Lucy's efforts have been remarkable, I agree, but she cannot understand the risk her new friends pose. And she must not learn the truth. She wouldn't understand. No, it's settled. This tiny TELLER and his scruffy CREATOR friend simply know too much.'

'And if the Guardians hear about this?'

'Armstrong and the others will continue to obey the rules. They cannot interfere. They're bound by contract, by paper and ink. A sacred pact. If they were to try something silly, well, they might suffer the same fate as Simon and Whippet.'

The man in the chair slumped even further into the leather. It looked almost as if he were part of the furniture itself.

'Humph . . . So what do we do till then?'

A wide smile spread slowly across the face by the window.

'The same as forever, dear chap. *I* tell the stories, *you* draw their pictures, and we entertain the whole darned WORLD!'

DEFINITELY NOT THE END!

COMING SOON . . .

Bazookas for Beginners

Lake Shore is safe for now, but where are the monsters coming from?

How much does Lucy Shufflebottom actually know? What does it mean to be a TELLER, like Simon, or a CREATOR, like Whippet? And what DOES Simon's dad do for work?

Simon and Whippet need some answers.

Will they find them when they enter CASTLE FEARLESS?

ROBIN ETHERINGTON, as one half of The Etherington Brothers, has written three graphic novels that have been nominated for an array of awards. He has also produced comic stories for bestselling brands like Star Wars, Transformers, Wallace and Gromit, The Dandy, Kung Fu Panda and How to Train Your Dragon as well as writing for animation and film. Robin regularly tours schools and book festivals with events in the UK and abroad. Through energetic, laughter-filled Q&A sessions he loves to share his passion for reading, writing, art and the power of imagination. *Freaky & Fearless* is his first novel series.

JAN BIELECKI has studied both comics and illustration and has co-created two critically acclaimed graphic novels in Swedish. He is also a prolific children's book illustrator and his work has been published in Sweden, the UK and France. He has illustrated the *Wrestling Trolls* series for Hot Key Books. He would rather draw than describe himself:

Thank you for choosing a Piccadilly Press book.

If you would like to know more about our authors, our books or if you'd just like to know what we're up to, you can find us online.

www.piccadillypress.co.uk

You can also find us on:

We hope to see you soon!